I0629865

# The Warrington Clan Book 1: Love's Whirlwind

Dr. Daphne L. King

ISBN:0692562095
ISBN-13:9780692562093

# DEDICATION

This book is dedicated to my family. Thank you for setting the foundation for me on how to love and live life with no limits.

**Family**

**They're not perfect,**

**My family.**

**Sometimes we fuss and fight,**

**My family.**

**They can be loud and boisterous,**

**or quiet and calm,**

**My family.**

**Their hearts are open,**

**My family.**

**Their hands are too,**

**My family.**

**Sharing and caring are what they do,**

**My family.**

Family is where we first learn to love and how to get along with others. Family and love are the central focus of Love's Whirlwind. This book will make you grab those that you love and cherish the time that you have with them and rekindle those warm, tingly feelings of your first true love. Sit back, relax, and enjoy the whirlwind of love in this story.

Happy Reading!

# CONTENTS

PROLOGUE ...................................................................................2

1 THE BEGINNING ........................................................................3

2 HOME ........................................................................................11

3 FAMILY TRADITION ...............................................................29

4 CHRISTMAS TIME IS HERE ....................................................33

5 GETTING REACQUAINTED .....................................................36

6 A NIGHT OUT ...........................................................................46

7 CRAZY MIXED UP LOVE ........................................................49

8 FAMILY TIME ..........................................................................63

9 LET IT GO .................................................................................69

10 A DAY AT THE SPA ...............................................................75

11 GIRL'S NIGHT OUT ...............................................................81

12 A LATE NIGHT AND EARLY MORNING ..............................96

13 RETAIL THERAPY ...............................................................109

14 BACK TO REALITY ..............................................................121

15 NEW YEAR NEW BEGINNING ............................................136

16 NEW ADVENTURES .............................................................147

17 THE MONTH OF LOVE ........................................................151

18 BITTER ..................................................................................164

19 VISIT HOME ..........................................................................166

20 ROMANTIC DINNER ............................................................174

21 THE FAMILY THAT PRAYS TOGETHER ............................183

22 GIRL TALK ............................................................................190

23 HAPPY HOUR ........................................................................193

24 WHIRLWIND .........................................................................201

25 IN THE EYE OF THE STORM ...............................................210

26 THE BEST LAID PLANS .......................................................212

27 IN THE STORM ......................................................................213

28 THINGS EXPLAINED AND SECOND CHANCES ................216

29 THINGS TO BE THANKFUL FOR .........................................230

ABOUT THE AUTHOR ..............................................................236

# ACKNOWLEDGMENTS

Fiction: Literature in the form of prose, especially short stories and novels that describe imaginary events and people. Literature that is a work of the imagination and is not necessarily based on fact.

The Warrington Clan Book 1: Love's Whirlwind is a work of fiction based on the imagination and creativity of the author. Any resemblance to any real person or situation is purely by coincidence.

The author hopes you enjoy reading this work of her imagination. Happy reading!

- A special 'Thank You' to my brother Troy for your support and 'Thank You' to my family for your investment in me and my dreams.

- Thank you to the best editor, Lynda Kemp at Collaborwrites.

- Thank you to my readers for your valuable feedback: Nicole, Jerri, Etta, LaTonya, and Renee.

# PROLOGUE

Theirs was a love affair that fairy tales are made of. But will love be enough for this relationship to last? Last December, Mila and Terrence were reacquainted with one another. They were from the same small Midwest town and their families had known one another for years. This meeting was purely by chance. Both had ventured out to the mall the day after Christmas. After accidentally running into one another twice in the same day, Mila and Terrence decided to spend some time together catching up. Their attraction to one another was instant and undeniable.

Mila was warring with her commitment to the relationship she was currently in and her intense attraction to Terrence. Terrence was contending with his broken engagement, his passion for Mila, and wanting to protect his heart from being broken again. Here is how the story began…

# 1 THE BEGINNING

"Life is so good! I am grateful to God for His many wonderful blessings. I still can't believe how successful my practice is and that I will have my own talk radio show next year." Who knew that the owner of the radio station sat on the board of the teen center where Mila volunteered her time in giving workshops on self-esteem to the girls that received services from the center as well as talking to them about maintaining healthy mental practices? "I'm so thankful that the owner of the radio station was so impressed with my knowledge about mental health that he offered me my own radio show! I have a passion for helping others live their healthiest life mentally and emotionally, especially those in the African-American community. What God has blessed me with will be used for His glory," thought Mila as she reflected back over the year that was nearing its end. "But she was at war with her commitment to her long-time boyfriend Brian and the diminishing feelings she was starting to have for him? She had invited him to come home with her to the Midwest for Christmas but he declined. Brian said he was going to just chill in his apartment since he couldn't go visit his family for the holidays."

Brian had grown distant since Mila signed the contract for her radio show making her one of the highest paid mental health professionals in the field. To top it off he was ten years her senior, they had been dating for four years and he didn't know if he wanted to get married at all. Mila had some decisions to make while she was home for Christmas. The buzzing of her cell phone jarred Mila out of her thoughts.

"Hey girl," it was her close cousin, Desiree on the phone. "What's up chic?"

"Nothing much. Getting ready for my flight home for Christmas. I can't wait to hang out with everyone when I get there. Girl, you know we must go to our favorite hanging spot. Oh, it is going to be so great!"

"I know. I can't wait either. How is Brian?" asked Desiree.

"Girl, I don't know what his problem is. I decided that I was not going to argue with him anymore about getting married. I'm not saying anything else," Mila responded.

"So do you think Brian is still upset about your not showing up to those functions that you were invited to at his boss's house?"

"I don't know. I've apologized repeatedly so I don't know what else to do." Mila knew the last six months she had been primarily focused on her career with negotiations for the radio show and then planning what her platform would be and how to market the show. She had not been as available to Brian to go on dates or attend some work functions that he felt were important to him. But throughout their relationship Mila had always made Brian a priority even when he refused to attend social events and activities that were important to her.

"So now that you've added the radio show to your schedule, how are you going to balance your time so that you show Brian that he is a priority? Desiree asked.

" Desi, I don't know." Mila replied using the affectionate nickname the family called Desiree. "I tried to talk to Brian about having one night identified as our date night where neither of us could schedule anything on that night but he refused. He said that he didn't want to become so routine in the relationship and that I needed to just make sure that I made our relationship a priority." Mila could feel herself getting exasperated again at the thought of that tiresome conversation with Brian.

"Oh okay. So, how did you respond to that?"

"I told him that I had always made our relationship a priority and that he was the one who declined invitations to attend social events and activities that were important to me. Of course, that led to a huge argument with Brian saying that I had become too career-focused lately, and that I shouldn't have accepted the offer for the radio show without talking to him first." Mila was completely outdone with Brian when he said that to her.

"Really? So, did he at least congratulate you on getting your own radio show?" Desiree couldn't believe that Brian was not supportive of her cousin's success with this new endeavor.

"Girl, he congratulated me and then quickly added 'but you should have talked to me about it first'. So, you know I reminded him that we are not married and have not even had a real conversation about a future together." Mila was starting to get mad all over again as she recounted that conversation with Brian.

"So, if you want to marry him why didn't you at least consult with him before you signed the contract for the radio show?" Desiree was proud of her cousin's accomplishment but Brian may have a point on this one.

"Because I told him when we first started dating that I wanted to expand on my practice and do more things with educating the African-American community on mental health issues. And because every time I tried to talk to him about marriage and us having a future together he wouldn't entertain the conversation?" Mila could be so hard on people sometimes and expect from them more than they are capable of giving.

"Okay. Ms. Therapist so why did you stay with him so long knowing that ultimately you wanted to get married?" Desiree inquired.

Laughing Mila replied, "Just because I'm a therapist and help others process their stuff doesn't mean I always handle my own personal life in the same way. I think after so many years I just got comfortable and didn't want to put energy into getting to know another man all over again."

"So what are you going to do now?" Desiree asked.

Mila replied, "after we talked in November and I asked him if he had thought about getting married and his response was, 'I don't know. It could be five years from now, it could be ten years from now, or it could be never' I decided that was my last conversation with him about getting married. I'm going to pray about it and decide what the best plan of action is for me. I am thirty-four years old. Life is not going to stand still while he decides if he wants to get married."

The Bible says, "he that finds a wife finds a good thing and obtains favor from the Lord," Desiree replied. "He has to recognize you as his good thing. You know we are a praying family, but don't use praying as a way to stall on making a decision. Make sure when God tells you to move or make a decision, you are being obedient to him." Desiree advised.

"Desi, I will." Mila knew Desiree was right but she didn't want to think about such things right before the holiday. "And then there is this family stuff. He completely flipped out when I asked him again about coming home with me for Christmas."

"Mila, how much do you really know about Brian's family?" Desiree knew the importance her cousin placed on family.

"All I know is that he was raised by some relatives because his mother died when he was very young. When ever I try to ask him more questions about his father and mother, he shuts down." As a therapist, Mila understood the impact the family of origin could have on a person's development and relationships.

"So you've never suggested that maybe he talk to someone about his family issues."

"Of course, I did, Desiree. But I can't make him do anything. He's a grown man. And, I don't want my professional life to intersect with my personal life like that. I can't date him and be his therapist."

"I realize that Mila but you also can't know this man has these issues and continue in this relationship with him. You know better than anyone how unhealthy that is."

"I know. Girl, let me call you back. My mom is on the other line."

"Okay. But really think about what I said," Desiree said.

"I will," Mila replied as she hung up.

Desiree's thoughts went to her cousin. She hoped Mila would use her good skills as a therapist to handle this situation with Brian in a healthy way. Desiree stopped and said a prayer for her dear cousin.

"Ugh... I HATE packing!" Mila always seemed to over pack when she was going to the Midwest for a long period. It was so hard to pack when the weather was so unpredictable there. It could start off decent and then a foot of snow will fall.

The ringing of Mila's phone halted her progress with packing. "Where is my phone?" Mila pondered. "Hey Brian. How was work today?"

"Hey babe. Work was work. Are you all packed?" Brian asked.

"Almost. I am finishing up now. I hate that you can't take me to the airport. So, we're not going to see each other before I leave?" Mila queried.

"I'm sorry too sweetie. I'll make it up to you when you get back." Brian promised.

"You know you could've just come with me." Mila offered.

"Your family is so big. It can be a bit much at times." Brian replied.

Shaking her head and rolling her eyes, Mila responded, "That is what family is for. My family is big but it is full of so much love and they have opened themselves up to you each time you have come to visit." Mila was starting to get irritated with Brian and this conversation.

"I know. My family is so small. I'm not used to that many people around all of the time." Brian was thinking that he didn't want to entertain this conversation again with his girlfriend. He wasn't ready to deal with his real issues surrounding family.

"Okay Brian. I don't want to rehash this again." Mila snapped. "I will call you and let you know when I make it to my mom's." Mila said to end the conversation. Mila was getting fed up with Brian.

"Babe, I love you. Have a safe flight." Brian really did love Mila but he had his own issues with family and commitment. He also knew at some point he was going to have to come clean with Mila about how his mother actually died and how he really grew up. He also knew that once her told her, Mila was going to do more than just insist that he seek therapy.

"Thank you." And with that said Mila hung up the phone. Her feelings for Brian diminished each time they had one of these conversations. "Brian makes me so pissed at times. This family thing is going to be a big problem for us. Family is important and my family is especially important to me. Yeah, I have a huge family but they are loving and can be very giving and generous. I wonder if Brian is really the man for me. I shouldn't have stayed in this relationship with him for these years." That thought became the defining moment for Mila and her relationship.

## 2 HOME

"This freaking airport is always packed. I really don't like flying into this airport but it has the most flights at a decent price for me to get home." Mila hurried to get to baggage claim. "It's so cold. I'm glad I have my fur coat with me. This is going to be a great Christmas! I can't wait to see my family." Mila could see Desiree's car coming down the airport lane. Desiree pulled up and Mila hopped in the car with her bags.

"Thank you for picking me up from the airport." Mila couldn't wait to get to her mother's house. She could already smell the cakes and pies baking in the oven. "Girl, you know Aunt Linda is in the kitchen doing her thing. I can't wait for those red velvet cupcakes to get ready. You know I got to sneak one when I drop you off." Desiree could already taste the delicious sweetness.

"HaHaHa.... You know my mom is not playing that. You know the rule. No dessert until Christmas dinner."

Laughing, Desiree replied, "That is why I said sneak. I can't wait until Christmas day for these red velvet cupcakes and I know we are not going to have any at the family game night tonight."

The two cousins left the airport and headed towards the highway to their hometown about an hour away. Family was very important to them and their relatives and they couldn't wait to celebrate this holiday with their family. Christmas was their grandfather's favorite time of the year. As the patriarch of the family, Mr. Warrington would make sure they had the biggest tree to decorate with more than enough gifts under the tree while ensuring that his family understood that the birth of Jesus Christ is the real reason we celebrate Christmas. He started the family tradition of everyone attending service together on Christmas morning and having one huge family dinner after church. Since his death the family continued to have huge celebrations during the holiday season.

Desiree turned down the radio so she and Mila could catch up. "Girl, guess who I ran into the other day?" Desiree was ready to do a little gossiping.

"Um well, I don't live here anymore and you didn't really give me any clues so I have no idea?" Mila responded with a questioning look on her face.

" Girl, Terrence. And boy was he looking fine." Desiree had a little twinkle in her eye at the thought of seeing their town's most eligible bachelor looking extremely good in his tailor-made suit.

"So who is Terrence?" Mila asked with confusion in her voice.

"You know Terrence. He played football back in the day and everyone thought he was going to play professional ball but he got injured in his last year of college and that ended his pro career before it got started." Desiree reminded her cousin.

"Oh. You mean the dude that was friends with Greg?"

"Yes." Desiree responded.

"What happened? I thought he lived in New York or somewhere on the East Coast."

Desiree turned down the music more and relayed the story. From what I hear, he was working in New York for this top Fortune 500 Company and decided to move back home after he was jilted by Regina before they could make it to the altar to get married. He has been back here for quite a while now.

"Oh. I haven't heard anyone mention his name in a long time."

"Yea, he and Regina ended their relationship some time ago. Come to find out she and Terrence had gotten engaged and one month after the engagement she just up and married some other guy. From what I heard, it was some guy that she randomly met in Manhattan while she was out spending Terrence's money." According to Desiree this had been the talk of their town ever since Terrence moved back home.

"You have got to be kidding me! Girl, who just ups and marries someone while they are engaged to another man?

"Girl, let me finish the story. Apparently, this guy may have only married Regina as some sort of revenge against Terrence for ruining his company or taking the company from him or something like that, and he wanted Terrence to feel the same sort of embarrassment that he felt from losing his company. From what I heard, the guy didn't even make a profit from the deal. He came out with just enough money to pay off some creditors with a small amount left over for himself. So, marrying Terrence's girl was the payback so that Terrence would know how it felt to lose something that you really loved. Of course, he didn't have enough money to support Regina in the fashion that she was used to with Terrence. This guy wanted Regina to get a job to help with household expenses so she totally went crazy on him and told him she was not the working type of woman. Financially, Regina realized that she had made a mistake so she divorced the guy less than a year after they married. Talk around town is that she recently moved back looking to get Terrence back."

Shaking her head, Mila said "what the hell? So, because her husband wanted her to get a job to help pay household expenses she decided to divorce him?" Mila could not wrap her head around this one. "Regina was always a little different though." Thinking about some of her behaviors during their childhood.

"Terrence was so embarrassed and hurt that he moved back to the

Midwest to regroup." Desiree continued with the story.

"Girl... That is a hot mess. It's women like her that mess it up for good women like us. I bet he is all bitter about women and has trust issues." The therapist in Mila was coming out with that comment.

Laughing Desiree said, "Okay so now you can diagnose his situation but you can't figure out what your boyfriend's issue is with his family?"

"See Desiree, you didn't have to go there. We are not talking about Brian." Mila snapped.

"But anyway, Terrence is really involved in church and I think Greg said he went to counseling with his pastor during that time."

"Well, I'm glad Terrence went to some type of counseling. It is nothing like prayer and the word of God to bring you through difficult times. Why is Terrence still hanging around here?" Mila asked.

"Girl, the company liked him so much and considered him such a valuable employee that they allow him to telework. He goes to New York about once a month for meetings and work related events. His money goes a lot farther here than in New York." Desiree replied.

"Wow... Talk about God's favor," responded Mila.

"The last time Greg spoke to Terrence, he said Terrence is thinking about leaving the Midwest and returning to the East Coast."

"Hmmm…" Mila thought out loud. "How fine did you say he was?"

"What do you want to know for?" Desiree asked.

"Just asking," Mila said with a smirk.

"I know you," Desiree told Mila. "Clean up and end the relationship you currently have before you start thinking about another man."

"HaHaHa... You do know me. It's just that Brian has been so distant and cold lately. I'm a very warm, giving, and affectionate person and it is heart breaking to be with someone that is cold and unemotional. And then, there is all this family stuff. He does not see the value in family. I am close to our family and family is very important to me."

"Mila, pray about it and actually make the decision God is telling you to make." Desiree advised.

"I will, Desi," Mila said. "Girl, how is your travel agency doing?"

"Girl, it is great! Business has picked up after folks started seeing the pictures of the trip I planned for the family last year to the Bahamas. I feel very blessed to be working for myself doing something that I love." Desiree beamed with talking about her business.

"Girl, I'm so proud of you. You know granddaddy sparked that entrepreneurial spirit in all of us with all of the various business ventures he had going on when we were growing up." Mila thought fondly of her grandfather.

"Yes he did and all those business ventures provided us all with the financial resources to go to college or start businesses of our own." Desiree said feeling thankful for how well their grandfather provided for his family.

"I agree. Girl, I know my mom's house is decorated and all lit up right about now."

"Aunt Linda's house is always decorated pretty during Christmas. And I know it's going to be smelling good with all the baking she is doing." Desiree replied with a laugh in her voice at the thought of her aunt's good cooking.

"Girl, it's going to be like the yard at homecoming at the house tonight. All the uncles will be there with their black and gold on. Then me and our younger cousin Leigh, will be there pink and green down. The icing on the cake is that our cousin Brandon took his butt and pledged a fraternity different from the one the uncles belong to so he will be wearing purple and gold." Mila shuddered as she thought about her uncles' reactions to this news.

Laughing so hard that she almost choked, Desiree squeaked out, "My dad and the rest of our uncles are going to kill him!"

"I know. I'm still trying to figure out how none of the uncles have found out yet. Brandon did a good job of keeping this one a secret. This fool also let them brand him. I just shook my head." Mila could not wait to see all her family this evening.

"Girl, they just got over him not attending their alma mater for college and now this. I'm getting to the house a little early tonight so that I can have a front row seat." Desiree was laughing so hard she almost swerved into another lane.

"Stop laughing before you hit someone." Mila cautioned her cousin. Brandon is not going to live this one down. Their uncles were very serious about family tradition and had a hard time with Brandon's decision not to attend their alma mater. Mila could not help wonder how they would respond to this news.

As they pulled up in front of Mila's childhood home it was like a scene from a winter wonderland. Their massive four-story house was decorated in beautiful crystal lights on the outside with small tea lights lighting the way up the sidewalk. In the front window were two beautifully decorated moving African-American Santa and Mrs. Claus dolls. The trees in the front yard were adorned with twinkling pink and gold lights. The lights hit the snow at just the right angle giving the illusion of being in a wonderful dream.

From the big bay window in the living room, Mila could see the most beautiful pine tree decorated in hand crafted pink, gold, and green balls with beautiful silk bows. Atop the tree the hand-blown china angel that had been in Mila's family for many years shone. She was hoping to one day have the angel on top of her tree. Ever since she had pledged her illustrious sorority her mother had been decorating the tree in some form of pink or green. It was absolutely breathtaking this year.

The scene brought Mila's grandfather to her mind. He was the true patriarch of her family and Christmas was his favorite holiday. "Thanks again for the ride Desiree. Girl, before I get out of the car, I meant to ask has anyone seen or heard from cousin Tim?" Mila's cousin had not been the same since he was in active combat in the war and would just wander off, not seeing or talking to anyone in his family for weeks at a time.

"No, and you know granny is very worried about him. It's like physically he has left the war but it's still one going on in his mind." Desiree knew the entire family was worried about their cousin.

"At some point, when he returns, the uncles should take him to the Veterans' Affairs hospital in the area so that he can receive the services he actually needs right now." As a therapist, Mila had frequently told her family that Tim was suffering from PTSD, which is typical for someone that was in live combat. No matter how much Mila tried to educate her family about mental health issues, it just seemed to go in one ear and out the other with some of them.

"I agree with you cousin. This time we actually need to take action and stop just saying that God will take care of Tim. Yes, we know that God is watching over Tim but He also wants us to put some action behind our faith." Desiree knew that having a relationship with God and regular prayer time was something that was instilled in her family by their grandfather as they were all growing up, but she sometimes felt that some of their family members just prayed without putting any real action or faith behind their words.

"Desi, you are absolutely right. Okay girl, let me get in this house and we will definitely continue this conversation about Tim later. So, you are no longer tempted to steal a cupcake, right? I don't need any help getting my bag in. See you tonight." Mila laughed as she said good bye to her cousin.

As Mila opened the door to her mother's house, she could smell the sweet aroma of her mother's famous cakes and pies. Mila's mother is known all over their hometown for her cooking. On an amateur level, she has catered wedding receptions, graduation parties, and dinner parties for people all over their hometown. But she will not take Mila's advice and start her own professional catering business. Her mother said that would take the joy out of cooking for her.

A poem came to Mila's mind as she surveyed the beautiful picture of her childhood home.

**Happiness is the smile that forms when memories arise.**

**Happiness is the smell of cakes baking in my momma's oven.**

**Happiness is the laughter of time shared with family.**

**Happiness is the satisfaction of a delicious meal.**

**Happiness is the feeling when time is spent with those you Love.**

Mila would write more later. Over the past year Mila had rediscovered her love of writing and poetry. She is now beginning to nurture that creative side of her. She was excited to greet her mother and grandmother as she was stepping into the main part of the house.

"I'm home," Mila shouted.

"Well, look what the cat drug in." Her granny commented. "Mila we heard the door a few minutes ago, what took you so long to announce yourself?" Her granny asked.

"Hello Granny." Mila gave her grandmother a big hug. "A poem came to mind as I walked in the door and I wanted to jot some of it down so that I wouldn't lose the words."

"Okay. Well, before you get to writing, check on your momma in the kitchen. You know your momma been in that kitchen all day. Are you going to help her?"

Chuckling, Mila commented, "Granny you know I don't like to cook."

"Yeah, but you do know how. Your mom's knees have been bothering her so you should go help." Granny was really good at giving out orders from her chair in the living room.

"Okay Granny." Mila respectfully responded.

"Mila," her granny called back.

"Yes ma'am." Mila responded.

"I'm real proud of you for starting to write again. You used to love to write as a young girl and I'm glad to see you pick it up again. Writing is going to be your way to heal the world." Granny looked at Mila with pride.

"Thank you granny." It felt good for Mila to hear that from her grandmother. "Hey mom. How's it going in here?" Mila inquired of her mother as she gave her mother a big hug even though she was all covered in flour. Mila looked affectionately at her mother and was so grateful that God blessed her with such a supportive and loving parent.

"I got all of my pies done but I need to take a rest before baking my cakes." Linda, Mila's mother said. Linda looked like she had been baking for weeks instead of a few hours.

Mila surveyed the scene in the kitchen. Flour covered the countertops and even made it down to the floor. Baking pans were lined up all over the table in the corner and cookbooks were open on the shelves across from the table. The kitchen felt of a sweet warmth with the smell of cinnamon and nutmeg. Mila breathed in deeply to take in the aroma.

"Mom, what happened in here. I've never seen the kitchen look like this before when you were baking?" Mila knew that usually her mom cleaned as she went along.

"I think I took on too many cooking jobs for others this holiday season." Linda was really tired but didn't want to let on to her daughter jut how tired she was.

"You didn't ask anyone else in the family to help you out?"

"No. You know how I am about my kitchen." Linda responded knowing that she was very possessive of her kitchen space.

"Okay mom. If you set all the ingredients out, I will bake the cakes." Mila reluctantly offered. "Let me put my stuff away and change clothes." Mila inherited her mother's great cooking skills but she had no interest in cooking. There were times when if something weighed heavy on her mind, Mila would bake to work through it. Baking was her therapy. Mila knew her mother did all the cooking for their family functions and sometimes it was too much for her so she decided to help her mother out.

Walking back into the kitchen, Mila asked, "Did you get the stuff for the cookies?" Her younger cousins loved to bake cookies on Christmas Eve to leave for Santa.

"Yes ma'am. I found that sugar cookie recipe you were looking for and bought new cookie cutters." Linda loved all things related to cooking, especially shopping for new cooking supplies.

"Okay. Thanks, mom. Michelle, Jade, Paige and Mikayla are always ready to bake cookies and leave them for Santa. What time are they coming over?" Mila knew it would be just a matter of time before her family descended upon them like a flood.

"I told them you could bake cookies at 4:00 before everyone starts coming over for dinner." Linda had the whole evening planned down to the final moment when everyone had to go home.

"Okay. That's perfect." Mila responded.

"How is Brian?" Linda asked.

"He is okay." Mila didn't want to get into this conversation with her mother today or any other day."

"Just okay?" Linda did not really care for Brian and now she was starting to get a little worried about her daughter.

"Mom… He's fine." Mila already knew where this conversation was going.

"Why didn't he come with you?" Linda always thought Brian was a little too nervous around people, especially her family. This made her very suspicious of him.

"He said something about wanting to spend the holiday alone since he couldn't go visit his family and our family being so big that it's overwhelming for him." Mila was bracing herself for her mother's over the top response.

"What is he going to do when you all get married?" Linda's frustration was growing with each question.

"Well... I don't know if that's going to happen. He doesn't know if he wants to get married." Mila cringed, "here it comes."

"You all have been dating for four years and he doesn't know if he wants to get married! He shouldn't have wasted your time these years," her mother shouted.

"Mom, calm down." Mila knew this was going to happen when they discussed the topic of Brian and marriage. "This is why I don't like talking to you about stuff like this. I'm going to pray about it while I'm here and decide what will be best for me." Mila was hoping this would calm her mother down.

"I'm sorry. I just want what is best for you," Linda replied.

"Mom, I'm confident it will all work out for the best." Mila was trying to reassure herself as well as her mother. Even as Mila said it, she knew that she needed to stop being at war with herself and make a decision about she and Brian. Mila had called Brian over an hour ago to let him know that she made it to her mom's house and he had yet to call her back. Mila was determined not to let her issues with Brian ruin her Christmas vacation with her family.

"Honey, how is Denise?" Linda hadn't seen Mila's best friend in several weeks.

"Mom, she's good. You know things have been a little hectic for her as superintendent of the school but she is enjoying her new position." Mila was very proud of her friend on this well-deserved promotion.

"Okay. I knew I hadn't seen her in a few weeks."

"I know I'll see her this break since we planned a spa day and I'm sure she will stop by the house while I'm here.

"Good. I made an extra dessert for her and want to make sure she gets it."

"Don't worry once she finds out you made her a dessert, she will surely make sure she gets it." Mila laughed knowing how much her friend loved her mom's desserts.

After a few hours of helping her mother in the kitchen and enjoying learning a few tricks of the cooking trade from her mother, Mila and her mother changed into clean clothes to spend this fun evening with their family. The Warrington clan invaded their family home like a tornado of fun and laughter. Mila had finished baking cookies with Michelle, Jade, Paige and Mikayla. Each had a platter of cookies to leave for Santa. Mila's mother had prepared a huge spread of food for their Christmas Eve celebration and with Mila's help had already started her dishes for Christmas dinner the following day.

Mila's family gatherings were also full of the best tasting food. This year her mother had prepared all comfort food. The table was full of mini turkey burgers, homemade French fries and sweet potato fries, garden salad, mini chicken tacos, buffalo chicken wings, homemade coleslaw, hummus and pita chips, tortilla chips and homemade salsa, sweet potato pie, and brownies. Everyone knew that the cakes were for dinner tomorrow.

As everyone delved into their second and third helpings, Mila found a quiet corner to do some writing. Her creative juices were flowing more these days.

They're not perfect.

Sometimes we fuss and fight.

They can be loud and boisterous,

or quiet and calm. Their hearts are

open.

Their hands are too.

Sharing and caring

are what they do.

Sunday family dinners.

Big celebrations.

Always a good time with fun

and laughter.

Worshipping and praising God is

What keeps my family together.

Love unconditional binds forever.

# 3 FAMILY TRADITION

The house was full of loud talking and laughter. The stuff that sappy holiday movies are made of. As usual Linda was playing her Nat King Cole Christmas CD, the kids were in the basement playing video games, and some of the adults had started games of spades and dominoes.

Then in walked Mila's cousin, Brandon, home from college. "Hey family," Brandon bellowed.

The whole house went quiet as Brandon's uncles, wearing their black and gold, stared in disbelief at their nephew wearing purple and gold. Black Greek fraternity/sorority life was a big deal and tradition in the Warrington family. It was expected that Brandon would follow in his uncles' footsteps and pledge the first Greek letter fraternity founded by black men on a college campus.

The disappointment showed on his uncles' faces. "Brandon, what have you done?" asked the eldest of the uncles.

"Uncle Brad, I pledged a fraternity this semester."

"I can see that, but why are you not wearing black and gold?" Hurt and disappointment showed on Uncle Brad's face.

"When I looked into the history of all the organizations, the

principles and ideals of this fraternity matched the values of my life."
Brandon was hoping this would be an acceptable argument for his uncle.

"We shared a lot of history with you on our fraternity as well as the reasons we all chose to proudly wear the black and gold of our fraternity. What happened?" Asked another uncle.

"I respect the legacy of your fraternity and the values that were instilled in me but we have been taught in this family to be an individual, to think freely and independently to make the choices and decisions that are right for us. " Brandon knew that this was going to be difficult for his uncles to accept. "Whew... I hope this class on debate I had this past semester pays off right now," Brandon thought as he was beginning to sweat under the questioning from his uncles.

"You were also taught about family tradition," Uncle Brad commented again.

"I respect and honor our family traditions, but I cannot pledge a fraternity based on family tradition alone. This is a lifelong commitment. At the end of the day, the black fraternities all work to better the African-American community," Brandon replied.

"We were looking forward to being able to share our experiences with you on the day of the founding of our fraternity as well as attend national conferences together." Uncle John commented.

"We can all share in being fellow members of black Greek-lettered organizations and the valuable work we all do in the community." Brandon replied to his uncle.

"We all were looking forward to pinning you as you became our brother and joined us in wearing the black and gold letters of our fraternity," Uncle Brad said with a look of disappointment on his face. "I don't understand you young people in today's society."

Brandon hugged his uncle and told him how much he respected him, but that the men of his fraternity were involved in service projects and community activities that were more in line with what he envisioned for his involvement in the community.

"Brandon, don't get me wrong, there is nothing wrong with the fraternity you pledged. We had just gotten over the fact that you did not follow in the footsteps of the rest of the men in the family and attend our alma mater for college and now this. But son, we will respect your decision," Uncle Brad replied. "But no more wearing purple and gold to family functions." With that Uncle Brad and the rest of the family laughed and resumed their activity.

Mila commented to Brandon, "You got lucky. They must be getting soft in their old age."

"Yeah. You know I was sweating bullets coming up in here."

Brandon could finally feel his heart beat slow down.

Laughing Mila said, "You made a very compelling argument counselor. I guess pre-law is the perfect major for you."

After Brandon greeted his granny and the rest of the family, the Warrington clan continued to eat and enjoy one another's company until late into the evening when the sky had turned a midnight blue signaling it was time for all the young children to go home and be put to bed to wait for Santa.

# 4 CHRISTMAS TIME IS HERE

Christmas day started with Mila, her mom, and grandmother enjoying a light breakfast before the family headed out to church. It was such a comfort for Mila to be home and attend her family church. It was nice for her to be surrounded by people who she grew up with and her family was so large that it always filled up one side of the church.

The church service was truly spirit-filled. As she sat in her pew, Mila asked the Holy Spirit to show up in the place so that God would get the glory out of their praise. The choir sang some of Mila's favorite songs —Silent Night, Joy to the World, and Hallelujah from Handel's Messiah. The pastor reminded everyone that the birth of our Lord and Savior Jesus Christ is the real reason why we celebrate at Christmas.

After greeting the pastor and his wife, and wishing their friends at Church a blessed Christmas, the Warrington family headed back to Linda's home for a Christmas feast. There was a smorgasbord of turkey, salmon, ham, crab cakes, dressing, macaroni and cheese, steamed vegetables, homemade rolls, collard greens, potato salad, more sweet potato pies, red velvet cupcakes, pound cake, and a caramel cake. Desiree was in dessert heaven as the sweetness of the red velvet cupcakes melted in her mouth. There was very little conversation as all present enjoyed the succulent meal that Linda prepared. By the end of dinner everyone was stuffed and ready for what is fondly termed, The Warrington Nod (a nap that is done anywhere – standing up or sitting in a chair).

Without fail, Denise stopped by to pick up the dessert that Linda had prepared for her.

"Ms. Linda, thank you so much for my dessert. I'm going to enjoy this with some vanilla ice cream as soon as I get home." Denise said as she gave Linda a big hug.

"Denise, are you going to share any of your dessert with your parents?" Linda asked.

"No ma'am. I'm going to hide this in my car until I get home." Denise replied as she was laughing because she most definitely was going to enjoy Linda's great tasting dessert all by herself once she got home.

"Girl, now you know you need to share some with your parents." Mila admonished her friend. "Tell your parents I said 'Hi'."

"HaHaHa!! I will not be sharing any dessert with them but I will tell them you said 'Hi'." Denise responded as she was leaving Linda's home.

Although she was enjoying the day with her family, Mila thought briefly that she had not heard from Brian all day. He was definitely helping her to make the decision she had been procrastinating about making. "Lord, this is not what I want for my life. I know what it takes to have a healthy relationship and I deserve a man who will love me and treat me like his queen," Mila silently prayed.

# 5 GETTING REACQUAINTED

"I'm a reasonably intelligent and educated woman, why did I decide to come to the mall the day after Christmas?" Mila was beating herself up over her decision. The mall was so packed and Mila hated being in crowds like this. Mila spent hours in the mall returning items for herself, her grandmother, and her mother who had both decided they were too tired to go out today. Finally, Mila was finished with all her shopping and returns and was leaving the mall.

As Mila was leaving the mall, Terrence was walking towards her. Terrence stopped dead in his tracks. He thought to himself that he had not seen a more beautiful woman. It looked as if the sun came down each day and gently kissed her. Her skin was beautiful and glowing. Where had he seen her before? She looked very familiar. She was breathtaking and just how he liked his women—tall and curvy. Her short haircut framed her face perfectly.

Terrence was so taken by Mila that he stood in a trance for a few minutes. Then it hit him, "That couldn't be Mila, Greg's relative. I haven't seen her in years and she does not live in the area anymore." Terrence was reminded that it was Christmas and Mila could be home visiting her family for the holiday.

Mila was so focused on the packages she had in her hands and navigating her way through the crowd that she did not even notice Terrence walking towards her. Her thoughts were on getting through the crowd in the mall as quickly as possible and out to the parking lot to her car.

Once she made it to her car, instead of driving home, Mila decided to stop at her favorite Mexican restaurant across the street from the mall. She decided to sit at the bar so that she could take advantage of the happy hour prices.

As he entered the restaurant, Terrence again spotted Mila immediately. Man, she is beautiful, he thought. As Terrence was about to grab a seat next to Mila he couldn't help thinking that this must be fate having seen Mila twice in one day. "Hello, Mila." Terrence greeted.

"Hey. Terrence, right?" Mila asked finding it ironic that she and Desiree were just talking about him a few days ago.

"Yes. Mila, it has been a long time." Terrence stammered.

"I know. I haven't seen you since you and Greg graduated from high school. You look good. What have you been up to?" Mila thought Desiree was right. This man is too fine.

"Not much. Just working. You look great! Life has been treating you well." Terrence stammered again.

"Thank you. I can't complain." Mila replied. "How was your holiday?"

"It was really good. The folks and I had a small dinner, and then my dad and I watched sports the rest of the day." Since Terrence's sisters were out of town, it was just he and his parents for the holidays.

"How are your parents doing?" Mila always thought Mr. and Mrs. Harper were just very nice, decent people.

"They are doing very well. Thank you for asking. They are enjoying spoiling their grandchildren." Terrence was thinking he wished he had children of his own for them to spoil but that plan had been derailed when Regina broke his heart.

As they continued to talk and eat, Terrence's attraction to Mila was undeniable. "Could he trust another woman again?" Terrence was thinking prematurely. He had just gotten reacquainted with Mila and he was already thinking about being in a relationship with her.

"So Mila, tell me what you've been up to in the last few years?" Terrence inquired.

"I'm a therapist." Mila replied.

"Okay. So, you get inside of people's head?" Terrence is hoping Mila is not one of those people that goes around diagnosing people just because that's what their profession is.

"Ha! No, but I do assist people in handling their problems in a healthy way so that they can come up with appropriate solutions." Mila had heard that comment about getting in people's head before when folks heard she was a therapist so she didn't think anything of Terrence's comment. "What do you do for a living?"

"I'm an executive in a company that buys smaller companies and turns them around to make a profit."

"That sounds very interesting." Mila did not know much about the business world. "Do you enjoy what you do?"

"Absolutely! I love it. I've always wanted to be in business and the company I work for has been very good to me." Terrence was proud of all that God had allowed him to accomplish.

"It's a great feeling to do something that you love." Mila understood this as she truly enjoyed being a therapist.

"Do you love being a therapist?" Terrence wanted to learn all he could about Mila while they had some time to catch up.

"Definitely! So much so, that I will be hosting a radio show about mental health." Mila could feel herself getting excited about the mention of her new radio show.

"Wow... That's great! Your own radio show... You always were smart and driven to succeed. What will be the focus of your show?"

"Providing mental health advice to teens and their parents as well as general mental health advice to those in crisis." Excitement rang in Mila's voice.

"That is really great! I wish you well in this new endeavor." Terrence was intrigued by Mila.

"Thank you. Good mental health is just as important as good physical health. Being emotionally stable is so vital to everyday interactions, especially those we are in relationships with." Mila hadn't meant to sound like she was giving one of her workshops on mental health.

"You are right there. I wish I had known that before my heart got trampled over." Terrence hadn't meant to add the part about his heart being trampled over but he found it so easy to be open with Mila.

"Well, I'm really excited about the new possibilities with this show." Mila ignored Terrence's remark about finding out the hard way. She was not going to analyze him but just enjoy herself while she was home.

While the two were getting reacquainted, Terrence's ex-fiancé, Regina came in with her friends and sat at a table near them in the bar area. Regina was confused as to what Terrence was doing there with Mila. "When did they start hanging out with each other." Regina thought to herself as she didn't want her friends to know that she was watching Terrence.

Meanwhile, Terrence wanted to get to know Mila on a more personal level. "Are you seeing anyone?" Terrence was showing his hand now.

"Umm.... It's a little complicated. While I'm home I will be making a decision about my current relationship." Mila answered sounding unsure at the thought of ending this relationship and having to get to know someone new all over again.

Terrence immediately thought, who is the man that was willing to lose this beautiful woman. If he had a woman like this in his life, he would never let her go. But then, he had thought something similar about his ex-fiancé and look what happened to that relationship.

"Terrence, are you okay?" Mila asked with a look of concern on her face.

The sound of Mila's voice woke Terrence from his musing. "Yea, I'm fine." Terrence stuttered.

Mila chuckled to herself realizing that she was the reason Terrence lost his train of thought and had been stammering through some of their conversation.

"Terrence are you dating anyone?" Mila couldn't help thinking again that Terrence was really an attractive man and she had been enjoying catching up with him.

"No. I'm not." Terrence had an uncomfortable look on his face. He didn't know if he was ready to get serious with another woman again.

"That's hard to believe. I'm sure the single women around here must be tripping over each other to get to such an eligible bachelor." Mila said with a little laughter in her voice.

"HaHaHa!! That's funny. I haven't found a woman that I want to invest that kind of time in." Terrence wanted to continue to talk with Mila. He found he was really enjoying the conversation. "Mila would you like to meet up later and continue catching up?" Terrence went out on a limb and asked although he knew Mila was currently in a relationship.

"Sure. That sounds like a plan." Mila responded without even thinking about Brian.

Terrence suggested that they meet up back at this same restaurant as they had a good dinner menu and the two only had appetizers at the bar. They agreed to meet back there later in the evening before going to a movie.

"I can't believe that Mila has grown into such a beautiful woman. The last time I saw her she was barely in her twenties and now she is a fully grown, sexy, attractive woman." Terrence thought, this must have been my lucky day to see her twice by chance. "I can't believe how she captivated my every thought today. My ex-fiancé never caught my attention the way Mila did today. Man, she is also very intelligent, funny, and completely charming. Without my knowing it, she has swept me off my feet. I don't think she even knows that she did it. I'm expecting to have a great time with her tonight. I hope we can have a nice evening without running into anyone that could possibly ruin it. I haven't been this nervous before a date in a very long time."

As Terrence was preparing for the dinner ahead, he thought, "Is this really a date or just friends hanging out and catching up for the evening? And, it sounded like Mila was already in a relationship. Mila said it was complicated. Is this dude stupid or what? He must not recognize the value he has in a woman like Mila. Dude better be careful because it sounds like he is on the verge of losing a really good woman." Terrence spent the next few minutes making sure he was dressed to impress while waiting to meet Mila.

On the other side of town Mila was in her favorite spot, in front of the mirror. "What am I doing? I shouldn't be going out or hanging out with Terrence or whatever I previously called it to convince myself it was okay to go. But Terrence is fine and he smelled heavenly! Wait, I'm in a relationship with Brian and I would be pissed if he went on a date with another woman." Mila was at war with wanting to go on the date with Terrence and knowing that she is still in a committed relationship with Brian. "However, I haven't heard from Brian. That jerk didn't even call to wish me a Merry Christmas!!"

"As each day goes by, the decision I need to make is becoming more apparent. I must admit Terrence is one FINE man and I found it refreshing to have a conversation with a man that wasn't forced and I also do love a tall man. He has the most beautiful skin, like he was dipped in honey and then kissed by the sun. Man, when I heard him speak it sent goose bumps up and down my arms. I don't remember his voice being that deep." Shaking her head Mila bit down on her bottom lip. "Terrence is very clean cut and well groomed, just like I like my men. The true test is how he is dressed this evening." Oh... Another poem came to Mila's mind. Here is what she wrote:

**Skin as black as the coals of Africa,**

**piercing eyes that shine like the light**

**of a new day.**

**Body rippled with taut muscles**

**that glisten from the sweat of**

**a long day's work.**

**A gait that sways with a rhythm**

**oiled by the beat of an African drum**

**and as smooth as pure ebony silk.**

**Booming voice that dips to the deepest**

**valley of the soul, sounding with the allure**

**of a well plucked guitar expertly played drawing**

**admirers from a far.**

**A voice that sends shivers through your body**

**as he speaks your name.**

"The man in this poem is truly a FINE one!!!" Mila laughed as she thought about the man who was the inspiration for this poem. Mila searched through her large suitcase for the perfect outfit to wear. She decided on a pair of dark washed, designer jeans that hugged her in all the right places. She paired the jeans with four inch, thigh-high, black leather boots and her fitted black sweater. She would top it all off with her favorite pair of oversized, sterling silver hoops and her black leather jacket.

As usual, Mila's make up was flawless. She settled on her signature smoky eye with nude lip-gloss and favorite rose colored blush. Mila gave herself the final stamp of approval as she stepped away from the mirror. "Girl, God's handiwork is awesome! You do great work Lord," Mila thought and smiled as she admired herself in the mirror. "What will the evening hold?"

# 6 A NIGHT OUT

As Mila walked out to the car she was driving for the evening she thought to herself, why am I nervous and I hope we have fun this evening. I have a boyfriend. I should not be nervous. This is not a date. When I get back to my home, Brian and I have a lot to resolve.

"Hey girl. I didn't see you pull up." Mila greeted her cousin Desiree who stopped by to see what food was left over from Christmas dinner.

"Mila you look great. Girl, you are too much. Where do you think you are going with those boots on?" Desiree knew her cousin had a love affair with fashion and designer clothes but she may have gone overboard tonight, and she still has not said where she is going.

"HaHaHa!!! Thank you. Girl, you know this is me. I love my high heels and I couldn't resist these boots." Mila knew she had a habit of sometimes going over the top with her love of designer fashion. "I'm about to meet up with a friend."

"What friend?" Desiree asked.

"Desi, I'm running late. I'll call you and tell you later." Mila laughed as she hurried and got in the car.

"Now she knows she is not getting away that easy." Desiree said out loud to herself as she picked up her cell phone to call her cousin.

"Hello cousin." Mila laughed as she answered the phone."

"So who are you meeting again? You know I was not letting you off that easy."

"HaHaHa... Desi, you are so nosy. So, I ran into Terrence today and am meeting up with him tonight."

"What?? You sure do move fast. So, have you decided to call it quits with Brian?"

"I haven't made any decision about Brian yet. But what I do know is that I'm not getting into another relationship until Brian and I end this one." That was one thing Mila was sure of.

"So when do you actually plan to appropriately end things and tell Brian of your decision?" Desiree asked.

"Well, I haven't heard from Brian since I've been here. So, I will have that conversation with him after the holidays." Mila was starting to get sad and tear up.

"What?" Desiree responded.

"Yeah. I called to let him know I made it and then I called on Christmas and have not gotten a call back. At this point I'm thoroughly pissed." Mila could feel the tears about to fall down her face but she was resolved not to cry and ruin the excellent job she had done with her make up.

"Wow…. It sounds like the two of you really need to resolve things before you do further damage and hurt each other more. What is his problem? Why didn't he call?" Desiree's heart went out to her cousin.

"Desi, I don't know but I'm too old to play games like this in a relationship. And he is way too old to be playing games." Mila was really starting to get pissed now.

"Alright Mila, don't focus on that tonight. Just go out and have a fun evening." With that said, Desiree hung up the phone and ended the conversation with her cousin.

Bobbing his head to some old-school Parliament, Terrence headed to the restaurant to meet the beautiful lady he was going to spend the evening with. Terrence was deep in thought. "Man, I haven't been this nervous before going out with a woman in a long time. But, why am I nervous anyway? This is not a date. We're just two friends hanging out together and catching up on old times. But, man, Mila is exquisitely beautiful and I am betting not like any other woman I have ever met. From our conversation earlier, she is a believer in God and is actively involved in the ministry of her church." What will the evening hold for the two reacquainted friends?

# 7 CRAZY MIXED UP LOVE

"Wow! Is this restaurant always this packed?" Mila asked.

"Yes!" Her companion for the evening shouted while laughing.

"You would think this is the only restaurant in town." Mila hated to wait for anything. She could be so impatient at times.

"It does have the best food and the ambience is nice." Terrence replied.

"You know I could eat Mexican food every day." Mila stated. "I love chips and salsa and shrimp enchiladas."

"Yeah and this place also has the bomb margaritas." Terrence responded.

The couple was finally seated and settled in to enjoy the good food and drinks.

"Mila, what are you going to order?" Terrence asked her.

"My favorite, shrimp enchiladas with black beans." She responded. "How about you?"

"I think I'm going to order steak fajitas." Terrence replied.

After the waitress came to take their orders the two friends continued with their conversation.

"So Mila, do you have any other plans while you are in town

visiting?" Terrence wanted to learn all he could about Mila.

"Denise and I will be having a spa day this week. Of course, I'll be hanging with my cousins and I would like to volunteer for a few hours at a shelter or food bank." Mila was also making sure that she actually gave herself some time to just relax and rest.

"Nice. So, you want to spend part of your time volunteering instead of just being lazy and enjoying the holiday?" Terrence was impressed.

"HaHaHa!! I will definitely be having a few lazy days but I do find some enjoyment in giving back and being of service to those that are less fortunate." Mila knew that helping was a gift that she had been blessed with by God and she actually enjoyed the times when she did volunteer at shelters or youth centers. It helped her to remember where her blessings come from and that God commands us all to help one another.

"Okay. I can respect that. Do you think you will have time for us to possibly hang out again?" Terrence wanted to spend as much time with Mila as he could before she left to go back to her home.

"I think that can be arranged. I'm having a really good time getting reacquainted with you." Mila was having one of the best times she has had in a while but that internal battle was raising its head with making sure she resolved things with Brian when she returned to her home.

Once their food arrived and the two tasted their delicious meal, conversation slowed down just a bit. A couple of margaritas and a delicious meal later, the two friends were laughing, talking, and having a great time.

"I can't believe that I'm having such a great time." Mila thought. "I haven't had this much fun in such a long time. Brian never wants to go out. He doesn't have any friends in our area and has not opened himself up to socializing with my friends. This is so great. But wait, should I really be out having this much fun with another man when I'm in a committed relationship? Ugh... Being an adult is full of so many decisions. I don't want to think about it. For the night, I'm going to continue to enjoy the evening and Terrence's company."

"Hey Mila, I remember this one time when we were in high school and me and the fellas stayed out too late so we decided to spend the night with Greg at your family's house. Every stair in your house creaked. We all almost peed our pants when we looked up and Mr. Warrington was standing at the top of the stairs with his belt in one hand and his gun in the other." Terrence commented.

"You know my grandfather didn't play."

Terrence admired Mr. Warrington as if he was his own grandfather. Mr. Warrington mentored a lot of the younger boys in their community and always opened his door to anyone in need.

"And you fellas were two handfuls when you were in high school.

"But, I never understood why your grandfather had a belt and a gun."

"Who knows? Granddaddy was old school when it came to stuff like that. He probably figured if it was one of his kids, he was going to beat them with the belt and if it was an intruder they were going to get a bullet." Mila smiled at the thought of the patriarch of her family. She thought often of her grandfather, especially at Christmas, since this was his favorite holiday.

The two friends continued to enjoy one another's company for the rest of the evening. The movie they went to see was a blur. The *Pursuit of Happiness* turned into the pursuit of something else. Terrence and Mila talked off and on throughout the movie. Some of the talk was about the movie and some was catching up on old times. The unassuming couple did not know that in the back of the theatre there was a vengeful woman watching them who did not want to see her ex-fiancé happy. Who knows what tricks she has up her sleeves.

The next day Mila slept in late. The sun glistening off the snow was her wake-up call. Yawning, she thought, "I had the most fun last night. I haven't laughed so much and so hard in a very long time. Today is going to be a lazy day." The knock on her bedroom door brought Mila out of her thoughts. "Come in." She shouted.

"Good morning Mila."

"Good morning mom," Mila yawned.

"It seems that you had a good time last night." Linda was hoping her daughter would offer her the information she wanted without her having to ask for it.

"It was fun. We just hung out and caught up on old times." Mila was wondering why her mother had this weird look on her face.

"Dear, you know you shouldn't be going out on dates with other men until this thing with Brian is settled. You don't want to start something new without properly ending the old one." Linda was not getting the information she wanted and did not want to start the morning off badly with her only child.

"Ugh... Mom, it wasn't a date. It was just two friends hanging out." Mila was about to get angry with her mother and she did not want to start this with her mother so early in the morning.

"Yeah, two friends, who have practically known each other all of their lives. How do you think that looks to people who might see you together?" Linda did not mean to sound as if she was scolding her daughter.

"Now I get it. Okay mother. Who called you this morning and

what did they have to say?" Now Mila was getting mad and her mother knew it.

"Why do you always assume someone told me something?" Linda started to raise her voice.

"Because you came in here this morning on a fishing expedition." Mila knew her mother knew she was smarter than that.

"One of the sisters from the church said they saw you out last night and they didn't know that you and Terrence were dating." Linda replied.

"One of the sisters from the church," Mila smirked knowing exactly who had called her mother. "For the record, Terrence and I are not dating. How can I date someone when I don't even live in the same state with him and have not seen him in more than fifteen years? We went out to catch up on old times." Mila could get so exasperated with her mother sometimes. These so-called sisters from the church were the reason a lot of young people didn't attend that church anymore. They were always gossiping or judging someone without getting all the facts first.

"Okay mom. I got it." Mila relented. "Changing topics, has anyone heard from Tim?"

"No. This is the longest he has been gone without contacting the family. I'm really worried about him and your granny is beyond worried." Linda said with concern in her voice for her nephew.

"Mom, when he comes back you all have to take him to the Veterans Affairs hospital for a full mental health evaluation. You can't take 'no' for an answer this time." Mila didn't want to sound like she was telling her family what to do but Tim could not continue without getting mental health treatment.

"I know honey. I think we all get it now. I know you have told us all this before but this time my brothers are going to step in and deal with Tim whenever he comes back."

"Okay mom. I'll continue to check in on this if he has not come back before I leave." With that said her mother left Mila lying in the bed. Mila dozed off to catch a few more hours of sleep. The vibrating of her cell phone jarred Mila awake. "Who is calling me?" Mila wondered. "I can't believe I slept half the day away."

"Good afternoon Brian." Mila had a bit of surprise in her voice as she had not heard from Brian since she made it to her mother's home.

"Well hello stranger." Brian responded.

"I should be saying that to you. I called you several times and even on Christmas and did not hear back from you." Mila knew she was on the verge of really giving it to Brian right now.

"I'm sorry. I ended up working through the holiday and then got caught up with contacting my family. I did call earlier yesterday but kept getting this message that said this subscriber cannot be located." Brian really just did not want to talk to Mila and have the same conversation about family and his not coming with her for the Christmas holiday.

"That's weird. No one else has had trouble reaching me on my cell phone." Mila said with skepticism in her voice.

"How's your vacation going?" Brian asked to change the subject.

"Fine. I'm having a great time. My family is so much fun to be around and we always have a wonderful time together." Mila smiled at the thought of not her family, but the man she spent the last evening with.

"I'm glad you are enjoying yourself. But you are talking about your family like y'all don't have your share of drama in that big ass crew." Brian knew that he was about to hit a nerve on that one.

"See. You need to stop and you know how I feel about you cursing in my presence. Families are big and messy and full of drama. But you love one another despite all of that. Even with the drama sometimes, we still love one another and have a great time when we are all together." Mila is on the verge of ending things with Brian right now over the phone.

"My family is not like that." Brian really did not understand how true family dynamics worked.

"I know. They are standoffish and cold and unloving." Now Mila was trying to hit a nerve with Brian.

"Hold on now. You are going too far." Brian tried to use his strong, paternal voice with Mila. He knew this was not going to work with her.

"Now you know how it feels to always have someone talk negatively about your family." Mila countered as she yawned.

"Why does it sound like you are still in the bed?"

"Because I am." Mila said.

"But it's one o'clock in the afternoon, Miss early riser. I only know of one reason that you would sleep late and you had better not done that with anyone else." Brian was beginning to sound worried now. He knew that whenever he and Mila went out she always turned heads. He knew one thing. She had better not be turning any heads or anything else while she was visiting in the Midwest.

"First of all, I am a grown woman and I can do whatever I want. Second, I went out with an old friend and we got in late. Third, do you think I'm the kind of woman that would do what you are suggesting with someone I am not committed to?" Now Mila was really fired up.

Brian knew it didn't take much or long for her to get really angry. Was he purposely trying to push her buttons? "See, you always got to take things to a whole other level." Brian was beginning to get annoyed.

"No. You said the wrong thing to the wrong person. You know me better than that." Mila's annoyance showed in her voice.

"Okay. Okay. I'm sorry babe. Things have just been stressful at work." Brian was trying to get her to calm down.

"You know. I think when I get back we need to talk and make a decision about this relationship. The last few months neither of us has been happy." There, Mila had said it and she meant it this time. She was ready for things to end between her and Brian.

"Speak for yourself. I never said I wasn't happy. You're the one with these grand ideas and need a change in your life." Brian knew when he said it he sounded insecure and scared.

"Really. Because I am trying to take my life to the next level and be open to all that God has for me, it is a problem for you? Maybe, you need to change the way you think and stop being an old stick in the mud." Mila knew she had gone too far with that comment.

"Here we go with the age thing again. You knew how old I was when you started dating me." Brian was growing angry as well.

"Yes, I did. But when we first started dating you liked to go out and do things. Now you just want to sit in the house and do nothing. We haven't actually gone out on a "date" in months," Mila countered.

"I told you, I don't like being out in crowds and spending all that money," Brian remarked.

"You didn't have to spend money for some of the things I wanted to do. Like my friend's birthday party, Dee's wedding, or the sorority function I asked you to attend with me." Mila was starting to yell now.

"I'm a mature, adult man and I don't have to go out and prove something to some people I couldn't care less about." Brian's annoyance and insecurities were showing.

"What are you talking about? No one asked you to prove anything to anyone. It's not about caring about other people but it's about caring about the person you are in a relationship with and compromising. I do it for you all the time. Do you think I wanted to go to all those parties with your corny co-workers? No, I didn't. I went because it was something that was important to you. But I never get that same consideration." Mila's voice and anger were rising with each word.

"Here we go again. And in the last six months you haven't gone anywhere with me that I asked you to, even when you knew it was events at my boss' house that were important to me. You know what, I don't have time for this." Brian replied.

"Seriously? I've already apologized numerous times for that. I'm not even going there again. I mean, are you even listening to what I said?" Mila asked. "You know what. Never mind. We'll make a final and firm decision about our relationship when I get back."

"Oh damn!! She is pissed again. Man, I can't get this right. Am I about to lose the only woman I have ever really loved? The only woman I have ever taken home to meet my family. I feel like she is moving so far away from me. It wasn't bad enough that she has a college education and I can't finish this one degree but now she has gone and signed a contract to have her own radio show next year making her the highest paid mental health professional in the field. How do I fit into all of that?"

"To top it all off, she has now gotten involved with her sorority again. She is hanging out and doing all this sorority stuff. Man, our worlds are moving further apart. Now, suddenly she wants to talk about our relationship and settle things with it. What does she mean settle things with it?" Brian really did not want to lose Mila but he just did not understand some basics of being in a relationship. "To add to that, I don't know how she is going to respond when she hears how my mother really died and the unstable conditions I grew up in. Especially, since she grew up in such a stable, loving family."

"Oh hell!!!!!! Brian makes me so mad sometimes. This is not what love is or is supposed to look like. Never again will I settle for less than

God's best for my life and that includes the next man I enter into a relationship with." Mila pulled out her journal and started writing.

**Find Love,**

**where?**

**High above**

**the clouds**

**down to**

**the depths**

**of our very soul.**

**Whose is it?**

**God's**

**God's Love.**

**Does not**

**cheat, lie, or steal.**

**Is not boastful, proud,**

**or lustful.**

**Never hurts or**

**causes pain, shame,**

**or embarrassment.**

**God's Love is honest**

**and kind**

**Humble and patient**

**Endures the test of time.**

**Makes me smile, not cry.**

**Makes me feel good**

**inside and out.**

**Let's me know I am His.**

**Love is found in God and**

**through God.**

**Let us Love one another by**

**first Loving God.**

"Lord, I pray that one day soon you send me a man who truly knows how to love the way you do. While I am waiting, teach me how to first love you with all my heart, love myself, and love the people that you have already placed in my life. Show Brian how to truly love the next woman that comes in his life. Lord, I need you to show me how to resolve this situation with Brian. In Jesus' name, Amen." Mila prayed.

Mila felt so emotionally drained after all of that. She decided to sleep for a few more hours.

## 8 FAMILY TIME

Mila finally woke up from a very late sleep. She lounged around the house in her pajamas for most of the day. As usual, her family has been in and out of their house all day. There was still plenty of leftover food that the Warrington family came to eat.

"Hey cousin. What's up?" Her cousin Leigh asked.

"Girl, nothing. Just having a lazy day." Mila responded.

"How was your date?" Leigh knew she was fishing for information.

"It wasn't a date. Who told you I went out? Never mind, I already know the answer. The people in this family are so nosy. By the way, we just hung out and caught up on old times." Mila knew she sounded defensive.

"Okay. Well. How was it?" Leigh asked again.

Laughing, Mila shook her head. "Girl, you are so nosy. We had fun."

"Terrence has always been a very fine man. Too bad he got mixed up with that silly girl and let her humiliate him." Leigh said while trying to get more information from her cousin.

"HaHaHa! Cousin, you are a mess. Speaking of fine men, how are things going between you and Christopher?" Mila was ready to shift the conversation away from herself.

"Girl, things are going well. Christopher has the same values I saw in granddaddy with treating women respectfully and actually courting me. We are enjoying getting to know one another and spending time together."

"I'm so happy for you. I can't wait to meet Christopher." Mila wished the best in this relationship for her cousin.

"Thanks cousin. I plan to bring him to meet the family real soon. Hopefully we can get our busy schedules worked out."

"Girl, please make sure that the two of you are making time to nurture your relationship so you don't end up in this mess like Brian and I." Changing the subject before Leigh could respond, "Hey, we should grab Brandon and hang out tonight," Mila offered.

"Cool. That sounds like a plan to me. We can meet at 'The Spot' for drinks."

"Okay. Tell the rest of the crew so they won't feel left out," Mila said.

"Alright. Is 8:00pm good?"

"Oh yeah. That works." Mila agreed. Mila spent the rest of the day lounging around her mother's home. It felt so good to have some time off work and be able to spend quality time with her family. Listening to other people's problems all day can be draining so having some time to herself was a welcome luxury for Mila. She was going to put all this mess with Brian out of her mind and enjoy the rest of her vacation with her family.

Mila was well rested as she prepared to hang out with her cousins for the night. She decided on a casual pair of jeans, a warm sweater, and her down jacket. The weather turned very cold and snow started falling. This was the Christmas winter Mila was used to. She and her cousins Desiree and Leigh pulled up to 'The Spot' to spend time with their close-knit cousins.

"Girl, tell me the real deal about your date last night," Desiree stated.

Laughing and shaking her head, Mila responded, "I'm saying to you what I said to Leigh earlier, you are so nosy. Just like the rest of the people in this family. Last night was just two friends hanging out and catching up."

"Okay." Desiree said. "I heard you two looked pretty cozy."

"Was everyone in town at the same place last night?" Mila questioned. "My mom came to me this morning with some nonsense that one of the sisters at the church saw us out."

"You know this is a small town and everyone knows everyone's family." Leigh responded. "You know people are nosy and think your business is their business."

"Girl, you know you are right. We had a good time and it was fun to hang out. That was it." Mila stated.

"Who all is meeting us tonight?" Mila asked Leigh.

"You know Brandon is going to be here. My sister Latasha, and I think Brandon's sisters are coming. You know it may just be the five of us as usual. Everyone else didn't want to come," Leigh responded.

"That's cool. We always have a good time when we're together. I can't wait to have a slice of this pizza. It is so good and I have been craving it for months." Mila replied to her cousin.

"Leigh, when are you leaving to go back to Texas? Mila asked her cousin.

"Tomorrow night. I have to get ready for a New Year's Eve gala I'm planning for one of my top clients.

"Okay. Girl, you are really doing it big with your corporate event planning business. I'm so proud of you." Mila said to her cousin.

"Thank you. I'm glad I finally found my niche and a career that I really enjoy." It took Leigh a few years to really decide where she wanted to take her career. "Since Desi has gotten her travel agency business off the ground, I'll be able to give her some business when the need arises for travel to some of the events."

"That's great you guys!"

"Thank you Leigh. I can't wait for us to start working together and build this corporate event planning/travel empire." Desiree was grateful for the business her cousin was going to throw her way. As they were finishing up this conversation Brandon walked into the restaurant.

"Hey. What up kin folk?" Mila, Leigh, and Desiree greeted in unison.

"Hey cousins," Brandon bellowed.

"Boy, you know you dodged a bullet the other night," Mila and Leigh teased their cousin.

"Despite what Uncle Brad said, you know they are disappointed about you pledging a fraternity other than the one they are members of," Mila scolded her cousin. "But you are right. All the organizations work to better the African-American community. But, did this decision have anything to do with that chicken-head girl I saw you on campus with not too long ago?" Mila teased her cousin.

"What girl?" Desiree and Leigh asked.

"See cousin. You didn't even have to go there. It wasn't about her. I really did my research and this organization matched my values and the commitment I want to make to the community." Brandon responded.

"What girl?" Desiree and Leigh asked again.

"Nobody." Brandon stated as he changed the subject. Brandon knew that these female cousins that he was closest to were not going to let it rest if he didn't change the subject. "Let's order some champagne and toast Mila on her upcoming radio show. Cousin we are so proud of you. Granddaddy's entrepreneurial spirit and drive to succeed lives on in all of us. Cheers!"

The cousins continued to celebrate as they laughed and talked about fond memories of their family. Several people they knew from their childhood came in and they caught up with them on old times.

As the night drew on, the cousins all realized that family is truly the most important thing that you will ever have in life. It was very late when the cousins parted ways, and they would see each other the next day at The Warrington home.

# 9 LET IT GO

In another part of town, Regina was fuming about her ex-fiancé going out on a date with Mila. Regina really had no grounds to be mad but she had let Terrence go before and she was going to do everything within her power to get him back. Mila, her family, and Terrence had no idea that Regina had been spying on them when they were out a few nights ago and was also watching Mila as she was out with her cousins. No one knew that Regina had been jealous of Mila since they were kids living in the same neighborhood and Mila just seemed to breeze through school where Regina struggled to just get passing grades.

The Warrington family was well respected in their town and it drove Regina crazy that everyone thought Mila was such a beautiful and smart person. "If that little witch thinks she is going to sashay into town and steal my future husband she has another thing coming," Regina hissed. "She has been such a little goody two-shoes nerd since we were kids. Thinking that she is smarter and better than everyone else." Regina's envy was growing with each thought of what she saw as she was spying. "Oh, I know they thought they looked so cozy on their little date. Terrence had the nerve to just gaze up in her face as if he had never seen a woman before. He was opening doors for her, pulling out her chair, and being oh so attentive. Oh, how I miss Terrence and the way he knows how to treat a woman like his queen." Regina was on a roll now.

"The only reason I said 'yes' to his proposal was because I knew he was going to make a lot of money one day and I have never been the working woman type. I went and messed things up by marrying that no good Lance, who turned out to have issues of his own and was only seeking some twisted revenge on Terrence. My job is going to be to win Terrence back," Regina vowed. With that, she was beginning to hatch a plan of deception and mischief.

"I think I will go on a little fishing expedition. Where is my phone? Good morning honey." Regina said as Terrence answered the phone.

"Regina you know I don't want you calling me. We have absolutely nothing to talk about," Terrence hissed at his ex-fiancé.

"If you didn't want me to call you then you should have changed your phone number or not answered your phone," Regina countered.

"I am not rearranging my life for you just because you don't know when something is over. We haven't been a couple for several years and there is no reason for you to be contacting me," Terrence was getting very annoyed with his ex-fiancé.

Laughing, Regina told Terrence that she saw him a few nights ago at dinner. "You two looked pretty cozy at 'The Place' a few nights ago.

I must say Mila has grown into a pretty woman. She was such an awkward child."

"Regina, what the hell are you talking about?" Terrence could feel his temper rising with her. Why was he even entertaining a conversation with this woman who had completely humiliated him? "Mila was never awkward as a child and she has always been a pretty girl. Anyway, how do you know what she looks like now you haven't seen her in at least fifteen years?"

"Oh honey, why do you constantly doubt me?" Regina questioned. "I was at 'The Place' a few days ago and saw the two of you there sitting together at the bar and then later that same night at the movie theatre. You were in such a trance you didn't even notice that I was in the restaurant too. You never looked at me that way."

"That's because you're not as beautiful, captivating, and charming as Mila." Terrence knew this would get a reaction out of Regina. "What were you doing, spying on us?"

"No, I just happened to go to 'The Place' with friends and I was captivating enough to get you to propose to me," Regina taunted.

"HaHaHa! Touché... But the best thing you ever did for me was to marry Lance and help me dodge a bullet by marrying you." Terrence was hitting all the buttons on that one.

"Oh so now you're hitting below the belt. You didn't think you needed to dodge a bullet when you asked me to marry you. You better be careful. That little witch is not all she wants people to believe she is." Regina was doing all she could to plant seeds of doubt in Terrence's mind.

Terrence was growing tired of the conversation and was about to put it to an end. "Why do you care? You never loved me and was only looking for a meal ticket because you didn't want to get a job." With a smirk in his voice, Terrence ended the conversation by stating, "You are pathetic. You have nothing going for you. You married some dude you barely knew and got divorced less than a year later. For the last time, I don't want you back and STOP CALLING ME!" With that Terrence hung up the telephone.

As soon as he hung up the phone with Regina, Terrence blocked her number. He also blocked her from his e-mails and social media accounts. Terrence also contacted his employer to ensure that no one from the company would put through any calls from Regina. He could not get over the nerve of her trying to dictate something to him. She has got to realize they will never get back together.

Meanwhile, Regina is at home pissed. "I can't believe that jerk hung up on me. He has got some nerve. I'm going to call him back. He doesn't hang up on me like that." Regina was surprised that when she tried to call Terrence's cell phone she could not get through. "He had my number blocked?!!?," Regina screamed. "I will try his home phone number. I don't believe this. I am blocked from calling his house as well." Regina tried all the other forms of contact to get in touch with Terrence. She was blocked from contacting him completely. Regina was thrown into a tizzy. She was going to get back at Terrence and Mila.

Shortly after the call with Regina ended, Greg called his boy to see what he was up to. "Hey dude, let's hang today?" Greg asked Terrence.

"Cool. Okay man. I am down to hang." Terrence stated. "Man, let me tell you about Regina."

Greg was confused and asked his friend, "You still having contact with Regina?"

"Man, NO! Terrence stated a little too loudly. "She called me today and basically said she was spying on me and Mila the other night at dinner. She started asking me questions about Mila. Saying that Mila is not all she wants people to believe she is. She was being her old jealous self. I hung up on her and then blocked her number from every form of communication I know."

Laughing, Greg responded, "Good for you man. Stay away from your crazy ex-fiancé. She means you no good man. Remember how she embarrassed you and how devastated you were to find out she married another man while engaged to you?  Don't go down that road again."

"I have no intention of doing that again."  Terrence assured his friend.

"Good.  I will pick you up in an hour," Greg stated.

"Alright man.  I already know the plan.  We going to get some food, a couple of beers, and then watch basketball all night."  Terrence laughed at how predictable he knew his friend to be.

# 10 A DAY AT THE SPA

"Girl, I'm so excited for our spa day." Mila cooed. "This was such a great idea. I can't wait to get my facial, pedicure, and full body massage. I've been so stressed lately. I need this pampering."

"I can't wait either. This school year has been very stressful and taxing. This day we will relax at the spa and then enjoy a great dinner at 'The Country Club.' You know the spa will serve you wine or champagne with your service. I know you enjoy a good glass of wine." Denise exclaimed.

"HaHaHa! You think you know me?" Mila teased her friend. "This is going to be a great day."

The two best friends finally made it to the most well-known day spa in their hometown. The spa was known for its excellent service and was an oasis of relaxation and wellness. Mila went into one room to start her facial while Denise went into another to start her massage.

As she was lying back to begin the facial listening to the relaxing sounds of waves, Mila was finally able to let her mind go and just relax. Mila thought of Terrence. "He has got to be the finest man ever and his voice is dripping with honey. I had a great time with him when we went out. It was so nice to have a man treat me like a lady and be so attentive."

What everyone did not know was that Terrence and Mila went out again after that first outing. They decided to go to Any Town (and yes, the city is really called Any Town. Some years ago, the residents of this small city decided to rename the city Any Town because they wanted people from anywhere in the United States to feel at home and welcome when they visited Any Town.) where no one could spy on them. Mila's thoughts turned to that evening. "We had such a great time hanging out at 'The BOB.' We laughed and talked all night like old friends should. He shared so much of himself with me and even told me about the humiliation in his relationship with his ex-fiancé."

"I have never had a man to open up like that and be willing to share and talk. It was so refreshing to be with someone and not have to beg them to have a decent adult conversation. And when he hugged me, oohhh... I felt like I fit perfectly in his arms. The night ended perfectly with the most electrifying kiss. Wow! It was almost like a fairytale. I know I'm not supposed to compare men but Brian never made me feel like this and I have not been attracted to him in a very long time."

"This facial is great!" Mila thought. "I'm glad Denise suggested a spa day. Things have been so stressed at work. It seems like people are filled with so much pain and come with a new set of problems each day. Now my schedule is going to be even more hectic with the start of my radio show. A facial was definitely in order. I can't wait for my massage. I so love being pampered," Mila said with a yawn.

In the next room, Denise too was relaxing and enjoying her services. "I'm so thankful to have a really good friend I can share things like this with. Our friendship has grown over the years and whereas we do not always agree on everything, we respect one another and value our friendship. This massage is great," Denise was thinking as the massage therapist went to work on her back. "I love being pampered and taking care of myself in this way." She also wanted to get the scoop on Mila's second date with Terrence.

Mila did not know that Denise knew about this. Of course, someone in their cozy hometown saw Mila and Terrence out together and asked Denise about it. She would get the story from her friend during dinner. Denise decided to just focus on the services she was getting and talk to her friend once they left the spa. The two best friends met at the pedicure chairs where they would be getting their final service. Both women enjoyed having their nails and toe nails well groomed and painted. The two women laughed and chatted, this was the perfect ending to their wonderful Christmas holiday. "Mila, what are you doing for New Year's Eve?" Denise asked.

"Girl, I'm having a few people over to my condo. I'm going to have some games and serve a few heavy hors d'oeuvres and drinks. Everyone is looking forward to it and I think we'll have a really great time," Mila responded.

"Oh, that sounds real nice." Denise exclaimed. "I think I'm going to go to church and then out to breakfast with the family afterwards."

"That's nice. Starting the New Year off in worship to God is a good way to ensure that you start the year off on good footing." Mila replied.

She could no longer hold it. "How was your date?" Denise blurted out in one big breath.

Mila looked puzzled. "Whom are you talking to?"

"You," Denise answered. "Don't even play coy with me. It doesn't become you and I already know you and Terrence went out on a date. Someone saw you two out together at dinner and asked me about it. This is the first opportunity I had to talk to you."

With a chuckle in her voice Mila responded, "We had a great time! It was refreshing to be out with a man who knows how to treat a woman and one I'm attracted to."

"So, Mila, are you telling me that you're not attracted to Brian?" Denise sounded confused.

"Girl, I haven't been attracted to Brian in well over a year." Mila had a sad look on her face. "I sometimes cringe when he touches me. I have tried to explain to Brian before that I need attention and I like going out and being active. Just sitting in the house doing nothing is not going to cut it for me. But, he just doesn't seem to get it. So, as time went on my feelings and attraction for him dwindled each day until there was nothing left."

"Mila, why did you not say anything before now?" Denise was really worried about her friend.

"I don't know. At first, I thought it was just me wanting too much and then the last six months I knew that I hadn't been as available to him with preparing for the radio show but then I realized that I had been giving him my all and not getting the same thing in return. I really tried to convince myself that I was still attracted to him but I couldn't fake it any longer." Mila looked so sad with tears in her eyes.

"Oh girl, I'm sorry you have been dealing with all of this." Denise advised her friend to pray constantly for God's direction and guidance. "Mila, you have to trust God and allow him to move in your relationship. He will tell you what is best for you and Brian."

"I know," Mila replied. "I have been praying and am making sure that I am listening to God's voice and his instruction. But I also know that with the praying I'm going to have to actually make a decision." Changing the subject Mila asked, "so how are things going on the dating front with you?"

"Mila, I've been so busy lately adjusting to this new job I haven't even focused on dating."

"Denise, make sure that you have balance in your life. Things can't be all work. You have to have some fun as well." Mila knew it was easier to give sound advice than follow it.

"I know. But I am going to a networking event at the beginning of the year so I'm expecting to meet some single men there." Denise was actually looking forward to getting out and meeting new professionals in her area.

"Well alright then. I will definitely have to get the scoop on that. Girl, I can't wait to have dinner at 'The Country Club.' I'm ready for some seafood."

With that the conversation ended and the two friends prepared themselves to leave the spa and head to dinner. A light snow was starting to fall as Mila and Denise made their way to 'The Country Club.'

# 11 GIRL'S NIGHT OUT

"Girl, this salmon is slamming." Mila smacked her lips with the taste of her favorite fish. Mila's meal consisted of grilled salmon, red skin potatoes, and steamed vegetables. She and Denise talked and enjoyed their succulent meals.

"Yeah. Girl, the food here is excellent." Denise smacked in agreement. "I think the chef here has cooked all over the world from France to New York to the Caribbean. I wish I could eat here more often. This has been a great day." Denise was going to hate to see her best friend leave in a couple of days.

"This has been one of the better Christmas holidays I have had in a long time." Mila's thoughts turned again to her grandfather, the patriarch of the Warrington family. He would have loved to share this holiday with all his family. Feeling herself starting to tear up, Mila directed the conversation and her thoughts in a different direction. "Girl, I am gearing up for a hectic schedule when I get back home." Mila stated.

"How do you feel about being on the radio with your own show?" Denise asked.

"I'm excited and a little scared. This is a huge undertaking and an even larger time commitment. I also want to make sure that I am giving sound advice and counsel to those that call in to the show."

"Are you ready for all of this?" Denise asked again.

"I am!" Mila said with excitement in her voice. "I love what I do and believe that good mental health is just as important as good physical health. I feel that God wants us to be healthy on all levels—spiritually, physically, and emotionally/mentally—and I want to do all I can as a professional to help each person reach that healthy level." Mila could feel the butterflies forming in her stomach.

"Well I'm sure you will do fine and I wish you all the best in this new professional endeavor." Denise toasted her friend.

"Girl, tell me how does it feel to be the new superintendent of the school system?" Mila asked Denise.

"Oh my gosh! Girl, one minute I love it and then the next I'm like what did I get myself into." Denise was really invested in the education of today's youth.

"Well girl, I'm proud of you. I know you'll be successful and will take the school system in a new direction to meet the needs of all youth." Mila was very proud of her friend.

"Thanks girl."

The waiter came back to the table to check on the friends. "Will you ladies be having any dessert?" the waiter inquired.

They both responded "No" in unison.

All the Christmas food and this delicious meal had the friends very full. Denise had a look of mischief in her eye. "So, back to you and Terrence."

Laughing, Mila said, "There is no me and Terrence."

"Well, according to the people in town, there is a you and Terrence."

Mila immediately took her thoughts to Terrence. "We had such a fabulous time when we were out a few nights ago. It was a perfect evening. The weather cooperated and the stars were twinkling at an angle where I thought I could just reach right up and touch them."

Denise asked her question a second time, "How was your date? Girl, where was your head just now?"

Shaking her head, Mila responded, "We had a great time! We talked almost all night. Terrence shared a lot about the situation with Regina and his healing from that ordeal."

"Terrence is a great guy." Denise exclaimed. "That was a hard time for him. He went through a lot of embarrassment and shame with that situation. If it was not for his pastor and his recommitting his life to Christ I don't know if he would have made it through."

"He sounded like he was still experiencing some pain from that incident," Mila stated. "I could hear it in his voice and see it on his face when he talked about his previous engagement. He must've really loved her. It's a shame that she did not recognize the gift God had given her in a man like Terrence."

"This is why we have to wait on God and allow him to guide our decisions." Denise thought about her own prayers. "I think Terrence ran ahead of God and it cost him a lot. Nevertheless, this situation allowed him to reconnect with God and learn from his mistake."

"That is what is most important. God knows that we are going to make mistakes. It is up to us to ask God for forgiveness and learn the lessons we need to from our mistakes." Mila felt like she was preaching her own sermon. The thought made her chuckle. "But, we had a really great time. I so enjoyed myself and it felt good to be with a man who was comfortable in social settings and did not mind hanging out. Girl, Terrence was so attentive. He pulled out my chair, opened doors for me, and even brought me a little gift. It was so refreshing," Mila thought as she was reminiscing.

"Wow... That sounds real nice." Denise hoped her friend was not getting too involved before she ended things with Brian. "Mila, be careful," Denise admonished. "Resolve your relationship with Brian before going any further with Terrence."

"Ugh… I know. This being an adult is highly overrated." Mila felt so unsure right now as the war continued to rage between her commitment to Brian and her intense feelings for Terrence. "I told Terrence all about Brian and what we have been going through over the last few months. We are just going to be friends and give me time to resolve things and be fair to Brian."

"Okay, girl. Be careful and pray constantly." Denise was glad to have a best friend that she could share her faith in God with.

The waiter brought the check and the two friends paid their bill and left the restaurant. They had a fabulous day. As Mila and Denise left the restaurant a slight chill had settled in the night air and a light snow was falling. The pure white of the snow cast a beautiful glow over the night. Even though it was small, Mila thought her hometown was beautiful. During the winter the snow cast the most amazing glow over the ground and during the summer, the sun would shine brightly on the beautiful blue water of Lake Michigan.

The ride home was a quiet one as the effects of the relaxing day were starting to hypnotize Mila and Denise. Soft jazz was playing from the CD player and the friends were enjoying the quiet and their thoughts. Mila's thoughts went to Terrence and how fine he was, and how she really needed to resolve things with Brian. A smile formed on Mila's face as she thought of Terrence. The ladies finally made it to the Warrington home.

"Girl, I'm so relaxed and ready to put my pajamas on for the night," Mila yawned. "I can't wait to get some rest tonight. My mother and grandmother went to visit my uncle and aunt for the day. I love my family but am glad to have the house to myself tonight." Mila also didn't want to have to hear her mother ask more questions about Terrence and Brian.

"Alright girl, go get some rest." Denise yawned herself. "Make sure you get some rest and don't have any late-night visitors." Denise laughed to herself.

"Bye girl." Mila rolled her eyes at her friend's statement.

Meanwhile, Terrence and Greg were at the sports bar enjoying wings and beer before they headed out for a night of game watching. The two had been friends for more than twenty years and had settled into a very comfortable pattern in their friendship. Greg's nephew Brandon joined them for the evening.

"Man, you know you dodged a huge bullet on Christmas Eve." Greg kidded his nephew.

"Man I know!" Brandon knew his uncles were still talking about his pledging a fraternity different from their own. "Terrence, man, I hear you and Mila been hanging out?" Brandon asked to steer the conversation away from him, already knowing the answer.

"You all talk about women talking a lot. The men in your family talk as much as the women do. To answer your question, we been catching up on old times like friends do that have not seen each other in a while, Terrence said.

"Whatever man. From what I hear it is more than just friends catching up," Greg responded. "You my boy but she's still my niece. So, you better watch yourself."

"Man you know me better than that. We are just friends catching up and getting reacquainted with one another."

"Terrence tell Greg about your date the other night." Brandon laughed knowing that only he knew about the second date between Terrence and his cousin.

"What date, man? I told you we just met up with each other by chance."

"No man. I'm talking about when you were in Any Town." Brandon was smirking now.

"How do you know we were in Any Town, Brandon?" Terrence asked.

"HaHaHa!! Because I saw you. I was over there hanging with some of my boys from high school and saw the two of you sitting in a corner looking cozy."

"We were just hanging out." Terrence was trying to hide the excitement in his voice as he talked about Mila. "We had a good time. We ate, drank, and talked about old times. Nothing more. Nothing less."

Greg and Brandon knew that Terrence was full of it and could tell that in this short amount of time he had developed a strong attraction to Mila. They both hoped that he would be careful and not rush things.

"Alright dude. We are going to leave you alone," Greg stated. "But we had some great times back in the day hanging in the old neighborhood. My dad was a cool man and liked having all of you hanging at the house but he didn't play. We all had a lot of respect for him."

The three reminisced about old times at the Warrington house and all the fun they had hanging. They also licked their lips at the thought of all the delicious meals that Linda cooked for them while they were growing up. With the sports bar about to close, the men left and headed to Greg's house for a night of game watching and more beer.

Sitting in her living room with a stiff drink in her hand, Regina was hatching a plan to get Terrence back. She refused to believe that it was really over between her and Terrence. Everyone deserved a second chance. She just had to make Terrence believe that she was really sorry. Regina also did not want to work and had never really been interested in getting a job. She had no problem living off a man. "I never should have betrayed Terrence the way I did. He is a good man and I'm sure would be a great provider. How could I have been so stupid?" Regina scolded herself. "Now, I have to figure this thing out because I absolutely refuse to get a job and I want all of the privileges that come with being a wife to a man with a good paying job like Terrence. I could try drugging Terrence. He never could hold too much liquor so I could slip something in one of his drinks and that would do him in. But how would I get close enough to him to slip something in his drink? I don't think he will ever let me get that close to him again."

Regina wondered how she got to the place of being this kind of deceptive and conniving woman. Something had hardened her over the years and she did not have the answers. She just knew that she had to protect and get back what was rightfully hers. In the beginning Regina did love Terrence. They had dated during college and fell into an easy pattern. Terrence was in college and Regina led everyone to believe that she was attending school in the same city as the college Terrence was attending but Regina was barely going to class and spent most of her time working on ways to get Terrence to propose to her since she thought he was going to play professional football. Terrence was so different from the guys she had dated previously. He was really sweet and very nice and she thought he was going to make a lot of money playing pro ball one day.

But then Terrence had gotten hurt at the beginning of his senior year season and was told that he would not be able to play ball again. Initially, Regina played the doting girlfriend and gave the appearance of helping Terrence while he was recuperating. But that got old quick and Regina realized that she did not care that much for Terrence. She went through the motions until Terrence got back on his feet.

Since he was a stellar student, Terrence was allowed to say in school on an academic scholarship. He graduated Magna Cum Laude and was admitted to an MBA program at Columbia University in New York. Regina had no prospects and no way of supporting herself and her relatives were tired of her mooching off them so she followed Terrence to New York. At first, the new adventure was exciting but soon Regina grew bored with sitting around all day and sometimes the night while Terrence was studying. Not to mention she found his friends in New York pretentious and boring.

"Why was all of this old stuff invading my mind?" Regina hated when she reminisced about her and Terrence. It brought up mistakes that she did not want to face anymore. "Oh... I hate that man," Regina yelled at the top of her lungs.

These bursts of anger and overwhelming sad feelings were happening more frequently these days and Regina was having more difficulty controlling her emotions. The move to New York was the turning point for Regina in her relationship with Terrence. Regina had always been insecure about her lack of education as school was difficult for her. She shied away from anything that had to do with academics and did not see herself as having any goals or prospects for the future other than marrying Terrence and his supporting her.

Once Terrence accepted the job offer with the top Fortune 500 Company in the country and they moved to Manhattan, Regina immediately started letting her insecurities take over and had frequent episodes of debilitating sadness where she couldn't get out of bed or periods of extreme feelings of being happy where she would binge and go on shopping frenzies. She couldn't handle the feelings of inferiority she felt at all that Terrence was accomplishing. This made her afraid that he would leave her for someone she thought more on his level. Regina was totally surprised and caught off guard when Terrence proposed to her. In her sick mind, she thought Terrence only proposed as a means to further his career by showing that he was a committed husband and family man.

Regina found a way to self-medicate so that she could function in the midst of the overwhelming mood swings and insecurity she felt. Spending most of her time in bars, Regina began to pick up with other lonely and sad men because she couldn't stand the feelings of inferiority that she felt when she was in the presence of Terrence's co-workers. Regina had convinced herself that she was no longer attracted to Terrence and never loved him. She reasoned that she was only going to marry him because she needed a man to take care of her.

She just didn't feel the same way about Terrence anymore. Love was not enough. Flying into a fit of tantrums, Regina banged her head against the wall to get rid of these memories. Regina knew that she should be taking the medication her psychiatrist prescribed but she couldn't drink and take the medication. She had also stopped going to see her therapist. She refused to give in to this battle between this sadness and emotional instability.

She was not going to accept the mental illness that plagued so many of the members of her family. No matter how much she banged her head she could not stop the memories. Terrence was really not that bad. She just didn't feel like she was good enough for him. Every time Terrence accomplished something at work or was given a promotion, Regina slipped further away from him emotionally and withdrew into her own self. She thought there was no way Terrence would want to stay with her since she did not have any ambitions of her own. She did not realize that Terrence loved her for who she was and didn't care about her level of education.

During this time, Regina picked up with that crazy fool, Lance. At the time, Regina did not know that Lance sought her out to find any information he could use to get revenge against Terrence. Lance would show up at one of the local bars that Regina frequented and became fast friends with her. Regina felt like she could be herself around Lance and did not have to pretend that she was smart. At first Regina and Lance started out as just friends with her talking to Lance about her insecurities with Terrence. What Regina didn't know was that Lance hated Terrence because of a business deal that ended badly for Lance so he saw this as an opportunity to get back at Terrence. Eventually, it turned into more with the relationship turning sexual between Regina and Lance. Things just clicked with Lance, and Regina felt like she did not have to be someone she wasn't.

Regina could remember the night she and Lance decided to get married. She had come to see him after leaving one of Terrence's work events where she felt dismissed by his colleagues. Regina could not talk about politics or investments or any of the things that Terrence and his colleagues discussed at these events. She went to Lance's place in tears after overhearing one of Terrence's female colleagues commenting to another co-worker about how she could not believe that Terrence was with Regina since it was obvious that she had nothing to offer him. All her insecurities came rushing back at her and after making passionate love with Lance, the two decided to get married. Regina believed that she and Lance were compatible and on the same level.

When Regina told Terrence she had married another man, she could see the utter devastation and humiliation in his eyes. She could also see that he loved her very much but now it was too late. She was married to another man.

In the beginning Lance was great. They had a few months of marital bliss before Regina found out that Lance not only had a drinking problem, but he married her as some sort of revenge against Terrence and did not have the means to support her as his wife in the way she was accustomed with Terrence. When Lance told Regina that he needed her to get a job to help with the household expenses she hit the roof.

Regina had never really worked before and felt that with the instability of her mental state she would not be able to hold down a job. Since, she had convinced Lance to add her name on his bank account, Regina had access to the little bit of money he had. Tired of pretending to look for a job, one day Regina went to the bank and withdrew enough of the money to purchase a train ticket back to her Midwest hometown and have a little bit of spending money until she figured out her next move. Not even six months later, Regina was divorced and back living with her family. She realized that she made a big mistake in leaving Terrence but was elated when she realized that he was also back living in their hometown. That day she decided that it would be her mission to get Terrence back.

"Oh my God... Why am I rehashing all of this mess?" Regina's tantrum had turned to melancholy and she was now sobbing uncontrollably. She needed to find the medicine her doctor had prescribed.

Regina finally found her pills and took the prescribed dosage. When she had finally calmed down, she was drenched in sweat and felt emotionally drained. When she flew into rages like that, Regina could not control what she did and often did not even remember the episodes. Regina was even more resolved that she had to get Terrence back because she could not get a job with these frequent episodes.

"If it is the last thing I do I will get Terrence back and we will get married," Regina exclaimed. "I just have to figure out how..."

# 12 A LATE NIGHT AND EARLY MORNING

"It felt so good to have a quiet house this evening." Mila stretched and yawned in fatigue. "I love my family but they can be a bit overwhelming at times. We are a very big and active family, especially around holiday time." Mila really wanted some time to herself without having anyone else ask her about she and Terrence spending time together. She knew that a decision had to be made about the relationship with Brian. Mila knew as a therapist, all the things that went into having a healthy relationship but somewhere along the line she focused more on helping others have healthy relationships and less on her own relationship.

The ringing of Mila's phone jarred her out of her dozing. "Okay. Who is calling me so late?" Mila wondered.

"Mila, how's it going?" It was Mila's mother Linda, probably checking up as usual.

"Hey mom. Are you and granny enjoying your visit with Uncle John and Diane?" Mila asked.

"Yes, we are having a good time," Linda responded. "We have to make sure we get your grandmother out and visiting her other children.

"When are the two of you coming back?"

"We'll be back before you leave on Sunday."

"Okay. Well continue to enjoy your visit and tell everyone I said hello."

"I will," Linda responded. "I was really calling to see how the spa day went with Denise?"

"Oh mom, we had a great time. The spa was awesome and so relaxing." Mila smiled at the thought of the day with her best friend. "You and I will have to go there on my next visit."

"Sounds like you and Denise had a good day."

"We had a great time and a blessed day," Mila said as she yawned.

"You sound tired." Linda commented on her daughter's yawn.

"Not tired. But, I am a little sleepy. Having a massage relaxes you and then we had a big dinner after that so I was getting ready to get in the bed when you called."

"Alright. I will let you get some rest. See you in a day."

"Okay mom. Goodnight." Mila thought about the call. "I love my mother but she can be so nosy some times. I know she means well and is a caring parent but whew... It can be a bit much." Mila knew her mother cared a lot about her and her good friend Denise. She only wanted the best for them.

"Okay... Why is my phone ringing again? I should've put it on silent." Mila was starting to get irritated with being wakened out of her sleep. "Hello," Mila said with irritation and sleepiness in her voice.

"Hey, Mila. This is Terrence. Did I wake you?"

"What's up Terrence? And yes, you did wake me. HaHaHa!! How was your evening?"

"I'm sorry for waking you," Terrence said with remorse. "I just wanted to hear your voice and my evening was fun."

"How sweet," Mila said with a smile in her voice. "You know, strange as it may seem, I thought about you a lot today."

Terrence could feel his attraction for Mila growing with each word.

"Why is that so strange?" Terrence teased.

Laughing, Mila responded, "Because I don't usually open up to or make myself that vulnerable to men I have just met. It usually takes me a bit of time to trust."

"Well. You just met your exception. I'm the likable guy." Terrence fell into an easy pattern of light banter with Mila.

"Wow... HaHaHa!!! You are crazy. I must admit there is something about you that is refreshing, that is not found in the men where I live." Mila was enjoying this conversation with Terrence.

Laughing, Terrence said, "For one, you and I are not strangers. We have known each other for years. We are just getting reacquainted with one another. Two, I was taught to respect and love women."

"You were taught very well. Tell your momma and daddy they raised you right." Mila said this with all sincerity.

"What did you do today?" Terrence asked.

"Went to the spa and dinner with Denise."

"Oh yea. I remember you saying before that you and Denise were going to have a spa day. How was it?" Terrence would make a note of this spa day to use as a future surprise for Mila.

"It was great. Very relaxing. Denise and I always enjoy going to the spa and it was a great way to get some pampering. After that, we had a fabulous dinner at 'The Country Club'."

"Man, you are a girly girl. Spa days and manicures and all that."

"You are hilarious! Yes, I am a girly girl. I love manicures, pedicures, and make up, anything glamorous."

"I can deal with that. I like a woman who knows how to be feminine." Terrence needed to be careful with his comments as his feelings for Mila were growing. Mila is still in a relationship.

Changing the subject, Mila asked, "How was your evening?"

"It was cool. The usual for Greg and I. Brandon hung out with us tonight. We haven't seen a lot of him since he started college."

Mila yawned and stretched as sleep was taking over.

99

"Mila, you sound like you're falling asleep." Terrence himself was getting tired.

"I am sleepy." Mila was yawning more now. "It was a long but good day. How about we continue this conversation tomorrow?"

"That's fine. Good night Mila."

"Good night Terrence."

The two reacquainted friends dozed off with thoughts of one another on their mind. The night was a peaceful one. The holiday season was filled with new promise for Mila and Terrence this year. Christmas magic was working its mojo on the two and their meeting seemed almost magical. Mila had not slept this well in the last few months and she knew it was because she was getting closer to ending this internal war with how to resolve her relationship with Brian. Mila felt like a weight had been lifted from her shoulders.

Brian was not a bad man but the problems in their relationship were causing Mila a stress she did not need. Terrence felt like he could finally love another woman again. He felt a sense of freedom after blocking Regina from contacting him. Mila and Terrence's dreams were consumed with thoughts of one another.

The sun shone beautifully off the morning snow. The glow of the sunlight woke Mila from a very restful sleep. "Mmhmm... I slept so well last night. Better than I have in months. I can't believe this is my last day in town before I head back home." Mila started to get a little sad, as she did not want to leave Terrence.

A knock at the door drew Mila out of her daydreaming. "Who is knocking on the door so early in the morning?" Mila hurried down the stairs to see who was at the door, thinking that maybe Terrence was surprising her. "Who is it?" Mila shouted as she opened the door. A surprise fell over Mila's face. "Regina what are you doing here?"

Looking tired and disheveled, Regina asked, "Are you going to let me in?"

"No." Mila responded. Noticing Regina's appearance and the crazed look in her eyes. Doing a quick assessment, Mila wondered if she would end up having to call the authorities to come and get Regina. "I didn't invite you over here and I'm not letting you in."

Anger showing in her face, Regina said, "You better leave my Terrence alone."

Mila was getting irritated at this foolish scene so early in the morning. "As far as I know Terrence is not yours and I don't know what you're talking about."

"Terrence is and always will be mine. I don't care what happened in the past," Regina hissed.

"Well, you probably should have been smart and held on to him." Mila knew she probably should not have said that given Regina's appearance and not wanting to antagonize her but her tongue was sometimes a little too quick.

"Look," Regina shouted as she thrust her finger in Mila's face. "Terrence and I will be getting back together so you need to leave him alone."

"You know what?" Mila's voice was starting to rise. "I'm not about to entertain this foolishness with you." Mila slammed the door in Regina's face, locking and setting the dead bolt behind her.

Mila immediately called her best friend, Denise. "Girl, you are not going to believe this."

"Oh Lord, what happened?" Denise sat up in bed.

"Regina just left my mom's house," Mila replied.

"Who?" Denise was confused.

"Regina, Terrence's ex-fiancé. She just left my mother's house."

"What was she doing at your mom's house?" Denise was getting concerned.

"That crazy woman had the nerve to come over here and tell me to stay away from Terrence because they were getting back together." Mila relayed the events of the morning to her friend.

"What? Are you okay?" Denise was about to head over to the Warrington home.

"Girl, I'm fine and am not thinking about Regina. I told her I was not entertaining that foolishness with her and slammed the door in her face."

Shaking her head, Denise told Mila she always did have a quick temper and acted so impulsively when someone pissed her off.

"I know," Mila said with some regret in her voice. "I got so mad at her audacity. There is nothing going on between Terrence and I and if it was it is none of her business."

Laughing, Denise told Mila, "Girl, you know you need to stop. You are a mental health professional; shouldn't you have a little more control over your response to foolishness?"

"What I know professionally doesn't always get used personally. Speaking of mental health, have you heard anyone mention anything about Regina displaying unusual behavior?"

"No, but you know Regina has always been a little different. Why do you ask?

"This is more than just acting a little different. Her appearance seemed disheveled and she had a far-off look in her eyes that I've seen in clients when they are manic." Mila wondered if Terrence had noticed anything about Regina's mental state when they were dating.

"What do you mean by manic?" Denise learned a lot about mental health from her friend during Mila's time as a therapist.

"It means that a person is cycling out of control with their behavior. It's usually seen in clients that are diagnosed with bipolar disorder. Their behaviors can be very extreme." Mila tried to explain this in a way that Denise would understand.

"Oh okay. I understand. But, I haven't heard anyone mention this type of behavior with Regina before."

After ending her conversation with Denise, Mila decided to place a phone call to Terrence. "Good morning to the most handsome man I know." Mila greeted Terrence with honey dripping from her voice.

"Wow. Good morning to you too. Mmmm… To what do I owe such a warm greeting?" Terrence enjoyed being awakened like this but was a little suspicious of this show of affection.

"Oh nothing. You have been so great to me since I've been home. I just wanted to show you that it is much appreciated and you are very handsome. HaHaHa!" Mila was enjoying teasing Terrence.

"It was my pleasure to spend time with such an exquisitely beautiful woman. You are absolutely breathtaking." Now Terrence was laying it on thick.

"Hmmm… I like the sound of that." Mila had a big smile in her voice. "I do have something that I need to share with you."

"Oh boy. This does not sound good." Terrence sounded a little nervous.

"I had a visitor today. Your ex-fiancé came by my mother's house this morning."

"What??!!??" Terrence got instantly angry. He was massaging his temples and shaking his leg as he usually does when he is about to get pissed about something.

"Yeah. She wanted to make sure I knew that you two were getting back together and I needed to leave you alone."

"You have got to be kidding me…" Terrence thought, Regina has gone too far. "Mila, you know that is the farthest thing from the truth."

"I know. I didn't give it a moment's thought," Mila replied. "I told her it was none of her business and slammed the door in her face."

"HaHaHa!!!" Terrence bellowed. "I know Regina was pissed. She has become such a jealous, conniving woman."

"Oh yes. She was absolutely pissed. I didn't care. I will not be intimidated and I did not invite her over to my house." Mila could hold her own ground in any situation.

"Beautiful, I don't blame you. Regina only wants her meal ticket back. She never loved me and proved that by humiliating me. I have grown so much as a man since that time, as a man of God. I didn't take the time to really get to know Regina and don't think she was wife material."

"Speaking of knowing Regina, did you notice anything that concerned you about her mental health state?"

"No. Not really. There were times where Regina would get really sad and not be able to get out of the bed but she always said it was because of hormones with her period. Why do you ask?" Terrence was a little concerned about this questioning.

"When she came to my mom's house this morning, she was dressed in a disheveled manner and she had a blank, glazed over look in her eyes. I've seen this look in the eyes of clients I have worked with."

"No. I've never noticed anything like that." Terrence was now thinking that maybe those extended periods of sadness were more than just hormones at that time of the month.

"Okay. I was just wondering. The next time around how do you think you will handle being in a relationship?"

"I will not rush a relationship again or be hurt like that anymore. My next relationship will be with a woman who I take the time to get to know better. The next time I will pray about the relationship and consult God before asking a woman to marry me."

"Wow. It is so rare to find a man that is so open about his mistakes and his relationship with God." Mila was amazed at this man on the phone with her. It is refreshing to talk to a man that can be so candid and open. Mila was truly being swept off her feet.

"You know had I not gone through my experience with Regina I would never have gotten to this place. Men, especially black men are taught to hold their feelings inside and not show any sign of weakness. But I have learned that this is in direct contradiction with how God wants us to be in our relationships. As men, we need to show the people we love how we feel about them and it is in our weakness that God truly shows Himself strong." Terrence surprised himself with that. "I guess going to Bible study and Men's Fellowship is really paying off." Terrence wondered if he had said too much.

"You are truly wonderful." Mila was in awe of what she just heard. "I think you are so right. If black men and women went back to the basics of loving one another and trusting God with their relationships, we would be in a much better space with relating to one another. Black men and black women have such a rich shared heritage. I wish we would appreciate and try to understand one another more." Mila was thankful for the examples of black loving relationships she saw in both her maternal and paternal grandparents.

The two realized that they had the same dreamy eyed view about relationships and the way black men should treat and respect black women. They talked for an hour or so before they realized they were both hungry and Denise was on her way over to see Mila.

"Mila, would you have dinner with me tonight? I would like to see you before you leave tomorrow." Terrence asked.

"I would love to but my family and I will be having dinner at my mom's house for my last night in town." Mila responded. "But you can come over and have dinner with us if you would like."

"That would be nice. I would like that very much." Terrence could not help smiling at the thought of seeing Mila this evening.

"Great! I'll see you at about 7:00. Talk to you later."

And with that said Terrence and Mila ended their conversation. Mila hurried to shower and get dressed before Denise arrived. She decided to keep it simple and put on a pair of jeans and a sorority t-shirt. Today was a day for lounging and saying good-bye until her next trip. Mila heard a knock on the door and assumed it was Denise.

"Hello, who is it?" Mila yelled through the door.

"Your stalker," Denise said laughing as she tried to disguise her voice.

"Silly, I know it's you and you're not funny, Denise." Mila opened the door for her friend. "I'm so glad you brought breakfast. I am starving." Mila could hear her stomach grumbling.

# 13 RETAIL THERAPY

Denise and Mila finished their breakfast and headed to the mall for a little retail therapy. "Take the shackles off my feet so I can dance. I just want to praise him," the two best friends sang as they cruised down the highway.

"God is truly getting the glory right now. He is so awesome," Mila exclaimed. Even as she focused on giving God glory, Mila knew she needed to listen to God and follow his instructions on the decision regarding her relationship with Brian.

"Yes. He is girl. I feel abundantly blessed by God right now," Denise proclaimed. "This is going to be a great year," Denise said with excitement in her voice.

"I receive that my friend. This is going to be our best year yet." Mila said to reassure herself about the decision she would make.

The two best friends continued down the road reflecting on how awesome God has been in their lives. The two beamed with excitement over the upcoming year and the shopping they were about to do.

"OMG!!!!!!" Mila shouted. "It is so packed in here. Did everyone decide to visit the mall on the same day? This is going to be an all-day trip."

"I think you're right my friend." Denise agreed as they walked into the entrance to the mall.

The mall was a flurry of activity, still packed with holiday shoppers trying to catch sales and good deals. Mila and Denise decided to just enjoy the day of shopping and each other's company without worrying about the crowd at the mall.

As Mila waited for assistance at the makeup counter, she found that internal war raging. On one side, she knew it was time to end things with Brian but just didn't want to use her holiday vacation to think about it and on the other side, Mila wasn't sure if she was ready to jump into a new relationship with Terrence. She thought Terrence was a wonderful man and she had been enjoying catching up with him while she was home but she was uncertain if she was ready to start something new when she technically hadn't resolved things with Brian.

A sales attendant finally became available. Mila was first on deck. She absolutely loved the makeup counter at any department store and today it would serve as a welcome distraction from thinking about the situation with Brian and Terrence. Mila decided to try some new, vibrant colors. She wanted a few more vivid lip and eye colors that were different from her usual nude or sheer pink colors. As Mila was finishing up at the makeup counter, Denise walked over with three new pair of boots.

Instead of leaving the mall, the two friends decided to take a stroll through the mall and just enjoy this shopping experience with one another.

"You look like you found some good purchases?" Mila asked Denise who was struggling a bit with the bag that held her new boots.

"Girl, you know I love a good pair of shoes and these boots were a really good deal." Denise loved shopping and looking good just as much as Mila did.

"Well, tell me just where do you think you're going to put another pair of shoes, let alone three pairs of boots." Mila knew that Denise had to convert one room in her house into a closet just to hold her shoes.

"HaHaHa! I know... I know... My shoes are already starting to spill over in the closet I just had built. But I'm sure I have room for a few more pairs." Denise responded while laughing.

The two friends decided to make a quick detour in the lingerie store to see what new items piqued their interest.

"So who are you buying new lingerie for?" Denise teased her friend.

"Me, myself, and I." Mila responded while laughing. "I want to look good for myself."

"Humph... You sure you're not trying to buy something to entice the good-looking Mr. Harper?"

"Girl, please stop. Terrence and I are a long way away from the lingerie stage. That's not happening until my husband and I say 'I do' in front of God and witnesses."

"Okay, girl. You are serious about this waiting for your husband? I've heard you say this a few times now." Denise was happy that her friend was growing in her relationship with God.

"Denise, I am. I've made so many mistakes in relationships before. I know that God doesn't want me to continue to bump my head against the same wall repeatedly." Mila knew that when she returned home she would make a final decision about her relationship with Brian.

Denise and Mila finished browsing through a few more stores in the mall. With their shopping complete, Denise and Mila headed back home.

"So, I invited Terrence to my mom's house tonight for dinner with my family," Mila said tumbling all of the words out of her mouth.

"Why would you do that?" Denise asked.

"I don't know." Mila was so confused about Brian and her feelings for Terrence. "He called me last night to say that he wanted to take me to dinner. I told him that my family wanted to have dinner with me tonight and he could join us if he wanted to. Of course, he said that he wanted to come. Girl, I hope that my family doesn't eat him alive."

"HaHaHa!!" Denise couldn't stop laughing. "You have done it now. You know what? Your family knows Terrence so maybe they'll go easy on him. How about I stop by for dinner to take some of the pressure off?"

"Girl, thank you. Dinner is at 7." Mila felt suddenly relieved. Denise dropped Mila off at her mother's home giving her a few hours to rest before dinner. Mila's mother and grandmother had made it back home from their visit out of town and the house was starting to smell with the sweet aroma of Linda's cooking. Mila drifted off into a deep sleep with thoughts of Terrence and Brian on her mind. Mila woke with a huge yawn stretching as she sat up in the bed.

"Oh my goodness," Mila exclaimed. "I can't believe I slept all that time. I must've been so tired. I guess all my activities the last few days and trying to figure out this thing with Terrence and Brian has wiped me out. I know that I must make a firm decision when I return home. If I were talking to one of my clients, I would ask them why they are procrastinating and advise them to make the decision that is best for them." Mila knew why she was procrastinating. She had grown used to Brian and didn't know if she had the energy to take the time to invest in a totally new relationship. "I know that things can't continue the way they've been between Brian and I but I'm not sure if I want to jump right into a new relationship with Terrence."

Sitting on the side of the bed thinking about this wonderful Christmas holiday and the action she would take in her relationship with Brian, Mila began to pray. "God, I really need to listen to you and follow your leading. Lord, I am asking you to order my steps and guide me in all my decision-making. Help me to end the relationship with Brian decently and without hurting him. Watch over my new friendship with Terrence and help me to not move too fast. Lord, I thank you for the time I've had to spend with my family and friends and I continue to seek you for everything. In the name of Jesus, I pray. Amen."

Mila felt renewed after her prayer to God. She got up and started to prepare for dinner with her family. Mila dressed in a cute pair of jeans and a sorority t-shirt for a casual evening with her family and friends. It was 7 o'clock and Mila could hear her family starting to arrive. Mila heard the chime of the doorbell and made her way to answer the door before any of her relatives could.

Standing on the other side of the door was Terrence. He was holding the most beautiful bouquet of pink roses and planted a kiss on Mila's cheek as he handed her the flowers. Blushing, Mila thanked Terrence and they both went to join the rest of the family.

"Good evening everyone," Terrence bellowed.

"Hello," the Warrington family replied in unison. Linda was shocked to see Terrence standing with her daughter.

"Well Terrence, you and Mila have caused quite a stir over the last few days." Linda watched for Terrence's reaction. She knew she may have crossed the line but was overprotective of her only child.

Stammering, Terrence said, "Um... I didn't realize anyone was interested in my spending time with Mila to catch up."

"From what I heard you two looked like you were doing more than catching up," Linda countered.

"Mom," Mila interrupted before things could go any further. "Terrence is a guest in our home and you have known him all of his life. Remember our conversation about listening to gossip."

The doorbell brought a welcome interruption to the conversation that was about to go in a direction Mila did not want. It was Denise. After greeting the Warrington family, Denise joined Terrence and Mila as she said "hello" to Linda. Linda excused herself to the kitchen to finish preparing dinner and set the table.

"Girl, I am so glad to see you," Mila whispered. "My mom was about to get started in on Terrence."

Laughing, Denise asked "What did she say?"

"It's not funny Denise. You know the usual stuff about people seeing us around town and it looked like we were doing more than just catching up with one another. But Terrence was so sweet. He brought me a beautiful bouquet of pink roses."

"Oh my. Where are they?" Denise asked.

"Let's walk into the dining room I put them in a vase in there."

"Oh… They are exquisite." Denise cooed over the flowers.

"Girl, I know. Brian has not done anything this thoughtful for me in quite some time. I love pink roses." Mila was starting to get caught up in the moment now.

"Snap out of it Mila." Denise cautioned her best friend. "You need to resolve things with Brian before you start up anything more with Terrence."

"Girl, I know. It has been so nice to be wined and dined over the last few days. But I prayed about it and I am trusting God to direct me in the decision He wants me to make."

"Okay girl. That's a good way to handle it." Denise was glad her friend had a strong relationship with God.

"Dinner is ready." Linda announced.

The elder uncle in the Warrington family blessed the food and said a prayer of protection and safety for his great-niece and then all assembled dug in to enjoy the tasty spread before them. You could hear a pin drop in the Warrington home as all those present were busy filling their mouths with Linda's good food and saving conversation for later. Linda cooked her daughter's favorite foods for her last night in town. There were crab cakes, grilled salmon, macaroni and cheese, a garden salad, and chocolate cake for dessert.

As they were eating, Mila caught Terrence staring at her several times. Mila welcomed the attention but did not know how things were going to proceed once she returned to her home. While the family was enjoying the food and one another's company, Regina sat a few houses down the street spying on the Warrington home.

"I cannot believe Terrence took that self-righteous little witch flowers. He used to always surprise me with beautiful bouquets of flowers. Not to mention that he is having dinner with her family when we never spent that much time with mine." Regina was starting to come undone now. She had not taken her medicine in several days and her drinking had increased. This caused her tantrums to come at a more frequent pace.

Regina sat in her car waiting for Terrence to leave the Warrington home. "What is he doing in there? They can't be having that much fun. If it's the last thing I do I'm going to keep Terrence and Mila apart. Terrence is mine and I'm not going to sit by and let anyone take him from me. Especially, someone who thinks she is smarter and better than everyone. I'm gathering all the information I need to win my Terrence back. This is just the beginning... Terrence will be mine again."

Inside the Warrington house everyone was winding up their stay and saying their goodbyes to Mila. After the last of the family had left and Linda and Mila's grandmother had gone up to bed; only Denise, Mila, and Terrence were left in the house.

Meanwhile, Regina was still sitting in her car waiting. "What is taking him so long to come out? Everyone else has already left what is he still doing in there? Oh, I think I see the door opening. Ugh... It's just Denise leaving." Regina decided to get out of her car after Denise left so that she could get a better look at the Warrington home.

Inside the house... "I thought they would never leave." Terrence said.

With a smile on her face, Mila inquired, "Why were you so anxious for them to leave?"

"Because I wanted to have some time alone with you." Terrence replied.

"Really... Hmm... Why is that?" Mila was being coy.

"Because I wanted to do this." Terrence grabbed Mila in a passionate embrace and softly kissed her lips in the most sensuous way.

Both Terrence and Mila could feel the passion growing between them.

"Mmm… Well, what was that for?" Mila was left breathless.

"Just for being you and sharing part of your vacation with me." Terrence was truly thankful for being reunited with Mila.

"Oh Terrence you have been so wonderful during my visit. I'm so glad we were able to reconnect and I have truly enjoyed spending time with you." Mila could feel herself growing hotter with each word.

"Mila it's obvious that we are attracted to one another and we have a lot in common. I just want to continue to get reconnected and learn more about you."

"Terrence, I just need a little time. I have to talk to Brian and resolve my relationship with him. There is also the distance between us. I'm not sure about having a long-distance relationship."

"Mila, slow down. Let's just take it one day at a time. I will give you some space to resolve things with your boyfriend. But I'm not going to let you go now that we have reconnected."

"Okay. Just give me a little time to end things with Brian but I don't want to rush into another relationship so we'll have to take this slow."

With that said, Terrence grabbed Mila in another passionate embrace that seemed to last forever.

Realizing that she was getting cold standing outside, Regina grew impatient with waiting and started walking towards the side of the house. "Okay so Denise has left so where is Terrence? I'm just going to walk a little bit further on the side of the house towards the porch and see if I can see anyone." Regina ended up looking through the big picture window that gave her a clear view of the living room where Terrence and Mila were standing and she saw Terrence grab Mila and give her a big passionate kiss.

Regina ran back to her car in a rage. "Ugh!!" Regina shouted. "If it is the last thing I do I'm going to stop Terrence and Mila before they even get started."

# 14 BACK TO REALITY

"All good things must come to an end." Mila felt a little sad as she prepared to board her flight and head back to her home. She had to think about the right words to say to resolve her relationship with Brian. First, however, she was going to sit back, relax, and take a nap on the plane. After about an hour Mila woke to the plane landing at the airport. After exiting the plane, Mila quickly headed to baggage claim to retrieve her luggage and hopped on the shuttle to the parking lot where her car was stored while she was away.

It is so beautiful here. The sun was shining brightly and it was much warmer than the frigid Midwest weather she had just left. Mila loved living in an area that generally had mild winters. She absolutely hated being cold and could do without the snow. New Year's Eve was going to be great tonight! Mila could not wait to celebrate with her friends.

"Ugh!! Even when it's not rush hour, traffic here is still bad!" Mila exclaimed as she proceeded down the Beltway towards Costco to pick up the food and other items she would need for her New Year's Eve party tonight. Mila had called Brian to let him know that she was back in town. Brian sounded aloof and told Mila that he didn't know if he was going to make it to her party tonight. Mila, initially was pissed but then realized that she did not care if Brian attended or not because being honest with herself she just didn't feel the same about Brian anymore. "I don't understand Brian. How is the man I have been in a committed relationship with for the past four years not going to come to my New Year's Eve party?" Mila asked to herself. "But you know what? I honestly rather Brian not attend. He wouldn't enjoy himself and that would just make me miserable and everyone else uncomfortable. Plus, this will make it easier for me to break up with him tomorrow and start the first day of the new year off with making a healthy choice that I should've made a long time ago." Mila thought to herself.

Mila's phone began ringing loudly in the car as she forgot that she had turned it up when she left the airplane. "I wonder who this is?" A big smile spread across Mila's face as she saw Terrence's name flash across her screen. "Hello," Mila said with a huge grin in her voice.

"Hey," Terrence responded. "I thought you were going to let me know that you made it back home safely." Terrence's voice showed his concern.

"I'm sorry," Mila stated. "I got so busy after I got off the plane with running around trying to get things ready for my party tonight. And then Brian and I had this huge fight so I've been a little preoccupied in the last few minutes."

"Oh, okay," Terrence responded. "Well, I'm glad you made it back home safely. How was your flight?"

Mila responded that her flight went well. "Do you have plans for this evening?" Mila asked Terrence.

"I'm going to go to church." Terrence replied. "Do you have everything set for the party?"

"No. I still have a few last-minute details to handle and then I'm going to rest for a bit until the party starts," Mila replied. "So, let me get off the phone and call you tomorrow and we can talk." With that, Terrence and Mila ended their phone conversation.

Mila made her usual phone calls to her mom, cousin Desiree, and her best friend to let them know that she made it home safely and then she continued with shopping for the party. "Oh my! Costco is so packed today! I guess everyone had the same idea of getting party essentials for the biggest night of the year." Mila thought as she shopped for her New Year's Eve party. Mila picked up various trays from veggie to cheese to sandwich platters. While she was there Mila also picked up a few bottles of wine and champagne to do a toast at the start of the New Year.

When she left Costco, Mila drove to Party City to pick up some decorations and noisemakers. Mila loved entertaining and couldn't wait to spend the evening with her good friends.

"I'm so glad to be home!" Mila exclaimed as she plopped down on her living room couch taking in the aroma of vanilla that always wafted through her condo from the big candle she kept on her bookcase. "I'm going to unpack and then take a quick shower before taking a much-needed nap." Mila loved visiting her family in Michigan with all their rambunctious family gatherings and being able to catch up with her cousins but taking a shower in her own bathroom with her custom-made shower head that gave the body the feel of a firm massage and sleeping in her big, queen bed with the memory foam mattress was something she could not wait to do. The comforts of her own home were something that Mila was so grateful for.

After her shower, Mila stretched out across her bed to get some rest before it was time to get ready for her party. The ringing of her cell phone woke Mila out of her sleep. "Hello," Mila answered not sure of what Brian could want after their earlier conversation when he said he would not be attending the party.

"Hello babe. What's wrong with you?" Brian asked.

"Nothing." Mila responded. "I'm just thinking about the getting ready process for the party and not sure of why you're calling since you already said you wouldn't be attending the party. What's up?"

"Nothing. I was calling to make sure you were all settled in."

"Yes. I'm home, unpacked, and lying across my bed until it's time for me to get ready for the party tonight."

"Okay. I wish I was there with you." Brian was trying to work his way back into Mila's good graces.

"Humph! If you wanted to be here, you would just be here." Mila said with sarcasm in her voice. "No, you really don't want to be here and actually, I'm fine with it."

"You know I have to work." Brian replied. "And what do you mean that you're fine with me not coming to the party tonight?" Brian was starting to get a little worried.

"You don't have to work until the morning." Mila fired back. "And I meant what I said. I'm okay with you not coming to the party. You wouldn't enjoy yourself and that would in turn cause me to not fully enjoy myself because I would be focused on that miserable look you wear when you are somewhere you really don't want to be."

"Oh wow... So, now we've hit the place where you don't want me around?"

"No, we've hit the place where I recognize that I like to socialize and be active, and you don't so I'm not going to force the issue anymore." Mila was feeling a sense of relief with finally coming to terms with her true feelings.

"Well, you don't have to socialize all of the time and leave me out." Brian was getting a little impatient with Mila and her constant need to socialize. He wondered why it could not just be the two of them.

"Brian, you are so ridiculous. I haven't left you out of anything but I'm not going to just sit around in the house with you anymore," Mila stated.

Brian could not respond because he knew Mila was right. He had gotten to this place of not wanting to socialize or go out. Part of it was his introverted nature and part of it was because he had insecurities from his childhood that he just never dealt with. Brian had never met a woman like Mila before and one that he loved enough to take home to meet his family, even with the risk of her finding out the truth. The thought of losing her was scaring Brian and he did not know what to do.

"Brian, I'm going to finish resting. I hope you have a good night and are well rested for work in the morning." Mila hung up the phone leaving Brian feeling like he had just lost his best friend.

Mila woke up feeling refreshed. "Oh sleeping in my bed felt so good." Mila felt like a weight had been lifted off her shoulders since she made the decision to break up with Brian tomorrow. Their earlier conversation sealed the deal and helped her to know what direction the conversation should take. Now, it was time to get dressed and enjoy the evening with her friends.

Mila decided to wear a floor sweeping pair of black palazzo pants with a silver sequin halter style top and her oversized silver hoop earrings. Her makeup was simple: silver eye shadow, a little blush, and pink lip gloss. Mila gave herself the stamp of approval as she admired her outfit in the mirror. The condo was decorated with silver lights all around. Noisemakers were strategically placed so that her guests could grab one as soon as midnight struck, and confetti was thrown everywhere to give the condo a festive look.

Mila set up the food in the kitchen and drinks in the dining area. There was plenty of food to satisfy the taste buds of all the guests. Mila's good friend and fellow therapist, Karen, arrived first. "Hey, girl," Mila greeted as she answered the door.

"Hey Mila," Karen responded. "Ooh... Everything looks great! I like how festive everything looks. We're going to have a great time tonight."

"Thank you. I just wanted to make sure that everyone has an amazing night and brings in the New Year having a fabulous time," Mila said as she gave the condo one last look before the other guests arrived.

Within the next twenty minutes Mila's other guests arrived and the

---

condo was brimming with people. Music was blaring, the television was set so they could watch the countdown to the New Year live, and the food and drinks were flowing. Everyone was having a better time than Mila expected.

Karen realized that Brian was missing so she pulled Mila aside to see what happened. "Mila, where is Brian?" Karen whispered.

"He decided that he was not going to come. He and I had this conversation earlier. He said he had to go to work in the morning so he didn't want to come. And I told him that I was good with that decision. I'm really not upset that he decided not to come." Mila stated matter of factly. "I will have to call you tomorrow to fill you in on the rest of the conversation. But basically, I'm going to break up with him tomorrow."

"What?" Karen shouted causing everyone else to look at the friends. Laughing, Karen replied, "It's okay. Mila was just telling me one of her funny stories."

Mila and Karen's good friend, Audrey walked over to where they were standing knowing that something else was going on. "What are you two over here scheming about. I know you too and that outburst was not about a funny story."

"Girl, you know you don't miss anything." Mila responded to her friend while chuckling at the ease the three shared in their friendship.

"Karen was just commenting on how Brian is not here and I told her that he didn't want to come and I'm fine with it. I also told her that I'm breaking up with him tomorrow.

"What?" Audrey whispered not wanting to draw attention to their conversation.

"Yes, I'm breaking up with Brian tomorrow. Look you two. I'm fine and at peace with this decision. Let's continue to enjoy the party and I'll tell you all the rest later."

Mila left Karen and Audrey to go mingle with her other guests. At the stroke of midnight, you could hear bells and whistles as the partygoers demonstrated their excitement as the New Year was dawning. The party seemed to kick it up a notch once they rang in the New Year. They ate, drank, played taboo, and had an exciting game of spades going. With the exception of Karen and Audrey, the last of the guests left at four in the morning.

"Okay, you two. I'm giving you the short version and then we'll discuss in more detail when we have our monthly outing." Mila knew these two were in suspense ever sense she said she was breaking up with Brian tomorrow. "So, you know Brian and I have been having our share of problems the last few months. I came to the realization that I have stayed with him this long because it was familiar and I just didn't want to put in the energy to get to know someone new."

"So, I knew you and Brian were having problems but this is new about you staying with him out of, what, habit or comfort." Audrey stated.

"Well, I think it has been that way for some time but with his reaction to my starting the radio show and our major difference about family, not to mention his not wanting to commit to getting married, I felt that it was time to really make a decision about whether to continue with the relationship."

"Girl, what does Brian think?" Karen asked. She had often felt that something was a little off about Brian when it came to interacting with others. It was more than just his being introverted.

"He thinks I should just not want to socialize and understand that my family is too big for him to be around. There is one other piece that I haven't told you. While I was home for the holiday, I reconnected with a family friend who is the finest man ever." Mila couldn't help smile when she talked about Terrence.

"He has to be fine for you to have that big grin on your face." Audrey and Karen both stated at the same time.

"Ya'll, he is. And it was so cool to spend time with a man that enjoyed being out and having fun. But, we decided to take things slow and not rush anything."

"Okay ladies, we will definitely have to finish this conversation later. I'm getting sleepy and want to be in my own bed." Audrey knew it was too late to have the conversation they really needed to have about this new information.

As the three friends said their good-byes, Mila assured them she would give them all the details on their monthly outing. Mila locked her door and settled in for a good night's or is it a good morning's sleep.

As she lay down to go to sleep, Mila's thoughts went to Terrence. He was so sweet and called her almost every hour to check on the party and wish her a Happy New Year. Mila couldn't wait to get to know Terrence better in the new year.

"Good afternoon Lord and welcome New Year!" Mila exclaimed as she opened her eyes to a new day and a new year. Mila stretched out on her bed still tired from all the festivities the previous night. Mila would have to get up in a couple of hours to get ready for the annual New Year's Day dinner at her good friend Evelyn's house.

But for right now, Mila was going to lie in bed until she felt well rested. Mila's phone rang off the hook the entire day with family and friends calling to wish her a Happy New Year. Mila spoke to her mother earlier that morning and Denise called to see how her evening had gone.

"Girl, we had a blast!" Mila said with enthusiasm in her voice.

"You do know how to throw a good party," Denise complimented Mila. "What are you doing the rest of the day?"

"I'm so tired. I just want to stay in bed and sleep. I'm committed to going to Evelyn's for her annual dinner. I can't wait! Her martinis are the bomb!" Mila was excited to continue the celebration with her friends later today. "What are you doing?"

"Actually, I'm having dinner with my family. I may stop by your mom's house later today to see what desserts she cooked.
"Girl, you know you are always welcomed at my mom's house and she and granny like when you stop by for a visit."

"So, you are not spending this holiday with Brian?"

"Girl, no. I decided to make a final decision about our relationship. Today, I'm going to call him so we can end things." Mila sounded so sure of her decision.

"What did you just say?" Denise asked. "It sounded like you said you're going to break up with Brian today?"

"I did say that." Mila restated. "I'm definitely breaking up with him today before it gets any worse." Mila didn't want to have such a heavy conversation with her friend today but it was time to stop procrastinating.

"Oh. I'm sorry to hear that." Denise was very concerned about

Mila. "That is too bad about Brian. I hope one day he works through his commitment issues so that he recognizes a good woman when she comes again."

"I feel the same way. I prayed for him when I was in Michigan and asked that God would show him how to love the next woman that he brought into his life." Mila would make sure she prayed before her conversation with Brian.

"Well girl, keep praying and enjoy your day today." Denise would also pray for her good friend.

"I'm going to do just that. Enjoy your family and tell your mom and dad I said, hi."

Mila's phone was going off again. "Now who's calling?" Mila looked at the caller id and could not hide her pleasure at seeing Terrence's name on her screen.

"Hello to a beautiful woman." Terrence was growing fond of Mila with each conversation they had.

"Hello to you too handsome." Mila was growing fond of Terrence as well. "How was your evening?"

"It was good. Church was on fire and then I had breakfast after church with Greg and Brandon. I'm so proud of Brandon for taking his education seriously so Greg and I wanted to spend a little more time with him before he left to go back to college. Greg is really growing in his relationship with God so we decided that we wanted to start this year off with God so that we could continue to grow as men and the leaders of our families." Terrence was hoping that one day God would bless him with a good wife.

"I'm glad you had a good evening. We had a fun time last night." Mila was still reeling from all her festivities last night. I'm proud of Brandon as well and am glad that Greg is following in my grandfather's footsteps with recognizing the need for an intimate relationship with God.

"Yea. That is what is most important. We get things wrong all of the time because we move ahead of God and don't trust him as we should." Terrence was really paying attention during Bible study and Men's Fellowship at his church.

"I totally agree with you. I know patience is something that God is working with me on. Each day I find something new and refreshing about my relationship with God and it makes me strive to be a better woman."

Terrence felt so blessed to have a woman he could share his faith with and receive encouragement from in God's word. He has to remind himself to take things slow and one day at a time with Mila.

"How are your parents doing?" Mila had a lot of respect for Terrence's parents.

"They are good. Enjoying that retired life. Thank you for asking."

"Good for them. They should enjoy life after working and raising a family. So, what is on your agenda for the rest of the day?" Mila asked Terrence.

"I'm supposed to go hang out with Greg today and have dinner with him at your mom's house but I think I'm going to pass on it and just rest today. I also need to go visit my mom and dad today. Both of my sisters went out of town for the holidays so I want to make sure they spend time with at least one of their children this holiday season."

"Oh okay." Mila replied. "I haven't seen your parents since your older sister got married a few years back. They looked good. Tell them I said, hello."

"I will. I told mom that you and I reconnected during Christmas and she mentioned that she saw you at Kim's wedding. Of course, she made it a point to tell me how beautiful you looked." Terrence was smiling as he said this.

Yawning, Mila told Terrence that she was going to rest a bit more until she had to leave for dinner and she would talk to him later that night.

"Okay beautiful. Talk to you later." Terrence stated with care and concern in his voice.

## 15 NEW YEAR NEW BEGINNING

"Oh my. I can't believe how tired I am. I didn't plan to stay at Evelyn's house so late but the food, fellowship, and drinks were awesome as usual." Mila yawned as she entered her condo. "I truly feel grateful that God blessed me with such a great day today and some special friends to celebrate it with."

Now, Mila was preparing to call Brian before it got too late. Brian answered on the first ring. "Happy New Year!" Mila exclaimed.

"Same to you." Brian responded.

"Thank you. Brian, this is going to be difficult but we need to have a serious talk about our relationship." Mila began this difficult conversation very cautiously.

"What do you mean have a serious talk about our relationship?" Brian felt that something was wrong but thought that he would have more time to fix things.

"You know Brian, I think we are moving in different directions right now. We don't see eye to eye about relationships and the value of family. I think we want different things from life right now. So, that we don't hurt one another further I think we should just end things now."

"Mila, I don't know what you're talking about." Brian was almost speechless. "I don't want to break up with you. I want our relationship."

"Brian, don't do this. You don't even know if you want to get married, how can you possibly say that you want our relationship. I can't anymore. Brian, it's time for us to end this relationship." Mila really thought the conversation was going to go a lot different than this.

"Mila, I will not lose you. I can't lose you."

"Brian, I don't want this relationship anymore. I deserve better than this and you deserve better than how things have been between us the last six months."

"Those things can be fixed. I'm not breaking up with you." Brian did not want to lose Mila. He just did not know how to fix things.

"Brian, it's time. I no longer want this relationship. It's over." Mila said to let Brian know that she was serious about ending the relationship.

"Mila, I need to share with you what really happened to my mother and it will explain some of the issues I have with family and commitment." Brian started cautiously as he was unsure how Mila would respond once he finished telling his story. "I know that I told you that my mother died when I was about eight years old and that is partly true. My mother was a very sick woman. She was abused for many years by her father and then an uncle. And you know back in those days, people just swept things under the rug so my mother was made to feel like an outcast in her family. "

Brian took a deep breath as he continued with the story. "So over the years she turned to men and drugs to ease the pain of the abuse she suffered as a child. Eventually, my mother slipped into a very deep depression. She attempted suicide several times and things seemed to just get worse."

This was the first time, outside of his family that Brian shared with anyone what really happened with his mother. "As a kid, I really didn't understand what was happening. Our family didn't provide any support to us and we were considered the 'black sheep' of the family so to speak. My mom kept a gun in the house because she was always fearful about someone breaking in. Well, one day after repeatedly watching her attempt suicide and hearing her tell me that if she could just sleep and not wake up things would be better, I killed my mother."

Mila was speechless. She had no idea Brian dealt with all of this as a child. "My mother had the gun in her hand again pointed at her head. She had been drinking and popping pills all day so her reflexes were distorted. She begged me to help her just end things so that she wouldn't have to suffer anymore." Brian could feel himself starting to get emotional but he was determined to finish the story.

"Brian, I'm so sorry you had to deal with all of this as a child." Mila said with tears in her voice.

"Thank you but there's more. So, I wrapped my hand around my mom's hand, which was gripping the gun. I put my finger in the trigger and pulled it for her. Blood was everywhere and within a split second my mother was gone. I called my Aunt Lois that you met and told her what happened. She came over immediately and called the police. She told them that my mother committed suicide and because my mother had previous calls for suicide attempts, there was no investigation. I spent the remaining years of my childhood motherless and being shuffled from one disgruntled relative to another." Brian was glad to have released all of that. He felt like a weight had been lifted.

"Brian, my heart really goes out to you. My gosh, I understand now why you feel the way you do about family. The very people that should have been protecting you and your mother as children, left you exposed and vulnerable. I am so sorry that all of that happened to you."

"Thank you. I struggled for years with telling you but it was just too painful to repeat and I thought you would think differently of me."

"Brian, none of what happened to you is your fault. But this is even more reason why we should definitely end our relationship. You should take some time to get professional help and heal without the added responsibility of being in a committed relationship."

"I thought once I explained to you what happened you would see that I just need some time to get myself together." Brian thought telling Mila the truth about his mother's death would buy him some more time with her.

"You do need some time but you need that time to yourself so that you can seek help without the pressures of a relationship. My feelings haven't changed. My decision to end the relationship happened before I knew any of this information. Now that I've heard this information, I feel that it is in both of our best interest to end things. But Brian, make sure that you go to counseling. You have a lot of things to sort out." Mila really did want what was best for Brian but she knew from working with her clients that the responsibilities of a committed relationship could be too much of a stress when you had your own issues to resolve.

"I don't agree and I don't want to break up with you." Brian didn't want to admit it but he knew Mila was right.

"Brian, my heart really does go out to you but let's not make this anymore difficult. It's over. But, please make sure that you talk to someone immediately about what you just shared with me." Mila did want to see Brian healthy and healed.

Mila said good-bye to Brian so that the conversation wouldn't be prolonged any longer. She immediately got down on her knees and said a prayer for Brian. She asked God to heal Brian from everything that he endured as a child and show him how to love himself so that he could be the man that God wanted him to be. Mila felt light and like she was being given a new start but also wanted God's best for Brian.

While Mila removed her make up she received several text messages from Terrence. Mila's face lit up when she saw the messages. But she was also worried about how Brian would fare in the coming days. "I love getting these little messages from him throughout the day." It was nice for Mila to be getting to know a man who appreciated her. Instead of sending a text message back, Mila called Terrence. "Well hello handsome." Mila enjoyed the flirting between she and Terrence.

"Hello to a most beautiful and sexy woman." Terrence enjoyed this and without he or Mila knowing, he was being swept off his feet. "How was your day?"

"It felt like it was so long. I had a great time at dinner. I just had a very emotional, difficult conversation with Brian. We just broke up with one another today and he has some real issues to work through and heal from."

"Are you okay?" Terrence asked, trying to show concern while doing cartwheels on the inside.

"I'm fine. I'm really at peace with the decision. I am a little concerned about Brian but I know this is for the best. I prayed about it and am trusting God with the decision that was made." Mila was confident in God and his direction for this situation.

"I can't argue with that. As long as you prayed about it and are allowing God to direct you then you can't go wrong. But I have to say that I'm not disappointed. I hope you are open to us getting to know one another better."

"I'm very open to that. I felt a connection to you at Christmas that I have never felt with anyone before. As long as we take things one day at a time and don't rush anything then I will be comfortable with it."

And here is how the whirlwind began....

Mila and Terrence talked to one another for several hours. Neither wanted the conversation to end. They talked about their families, growing up in the Midwest, and the direction their lives had taken them as adults. Terrence thought about how he had never felt this connection with any woman before and had never shared so much so soon with anyone. Mila was being her usual cautious self but found that she felt like she could trust Terrence and enjoyed hearing his voice.

After a few more hours on the telephone, Terrence and Mila realized that they were both tired so they ended their conversation and drifted off to dreams of one another. Mila slept late into the morning since she had the day off. She woke with a big yawn and stretch. "I think I'm going to just lay here for a while," Mila stated. "I'm not ready to get up yet. This is going to be my lazy day." Mila drifted back off to get a few more hours of sleep.

Mila's vibrating cell phone jarred her out of a very sound sleep. "Who could be calling me at this hour?" Mila looked at her clock and saw that it was one o'clock in the afternoon. "Oh my, I didn't realize that I had slept so late. Hello?" Mila still had sleep in her voice.

"Hey girl." It was Denise. "I know you are not still asleep?"

"Girl, I just woke up. I figured since I wasn't working today I would just relax and take it easy."

"What did you do last night? Did you have a late night?"

"I went to Evelyn's for dinner and as usual we stayed there very late with talking and fellowshipping. Then I came home to a very heavy conversation with Brian. Bottom line, we broke up and Brian has some things that he should work through in therapy. After that, I spent the rest of the night talking to Terrence."

"Wow.... Are you okay about the break up?" Denise was very concerned about her friend.

"I'm okay. For some time, I knew that my feelings for Brian had changed and it wasn't enough to stay in a relationship with someone just because it was comfortable. And with our differences about family and marriage, breaking up was the right thing to do for both of us. I prayed about it and felt lighter and relieved after the conversation. I'm actually good with the decision."

"Oh I'm so sorry. But, you're right. You have to do what is best for you and not settle for less than God's best." Denise was very sorry for her friend and only wanted to see her happy. "So, where does that leave things with you and Terrence?"

"Girl, we like each other and really connected. I told him that I want to take things one day at a time. I don't want to rush things." Mila was smiling on the inside as she thought about Terrence. "We'll see how things go."

"So, what's going on with you?" Mila didn't want to seem like she was hogging the conversation talking about herself.

"Girl, nothing much. I'm just relaxing as well and enjoying the time off before school opens again."

"Okay. Make sure you take some time for you because you know that once work starts back up you have a one-track mind."

"HaHaHa... I know. I set a goal for myself in the new year to make sure that I get out to at least one networking or fun activity a month."

"Good. I like the sound of that. Take some time to just have fun once in a while."

Mila finally got out of the bed and started to move about. She made herself a big breakfast of scrambled eggs, bagel and cream cheese, and a veggie sausage patty. She watched her favorite channel showing classic movies while she ate. They were running a marathon of Betty Davis movies. Mila was going to watch *Jezebel, Now Voyager,* and *What Happened to Baby Jane.* She absolutely loved the classic movies. The glamour of the "Golden" era of Hollywood always appealed to Mila's ultra-feminine side.

During the second movie, Mila's cell phone vibrated again. It was her mother. "Oh shoot, I'm not ready for a conversation with my mother." Mila was nervous about answering this call. "I hope she doesn't ask me about Brian. Hey mom. What's up?"

"Nothing." Linda replied. "I was just seeing what you were up to."

"Just sitting on the couch." Mila stated. "I'm watching a Betty Davis marathon on the classic movie channel and eating breakfast."

"Oh. That sounds like a very relaxing day. Are you alone?" Linda was fishing for information again.

"Here we go." Mila thought. "Mom, what are you trying to ask me? And yes, I'm alone."

"I thought maybe Brian would be over visiting."

"No mom. Brian is not over visiting and I doubt he will be visiting any time soon since we broke up."

"Uh oh… What happened?"

"Nothing new. We're just at difference places in life right now and

I've known for some time that I wasn't really happy in the relationship with Brian."

"I'm sorry to hear that honey. Are you okay?"

"Yes, mom. I'm actually fine. I prayed about it and I know that God has something better for me."

"Well okay. All right, I was just checking on you."

"What are you and granny doing today?" Mila asked to change the topic of conversation.

"Your grandmother and I are getting ready to head to the church to help with sorting items to be donated to the shelter."

"Oh nice. That sounds like a productive way for the two of you to spend your time. Tell granny I said, Hi." Mila was relieved, "That went better than I thought it would."

She put her cell phone on silent and resumed watching her movie marathon. Once the movie marathon ended, Mila began preparing for her week. She needed to fix her lunch for work tomorrow and begin to get her notes ready, as this was the week that she would start her radio show. Mila was getting excited at the thought of this new adventure.

Tomorrow would also start the fast that she did at the beginning of each year to prepare her heart, mind, and soul to hear from God. Mila knew that this year was going to be an awesome year in her life.

# 16 NEW ADVENTURES

The week at work was moving along rather quickly. The week was filled with numerous meetings and co-facilitating groups with the clients that she served. By Friday, Mila was wiped out but had to get her second wind as she headed to the radio station after work at the private practice. Mila did not know if she would make it to 9:00 p.m. The radio show would focus on healthy ways to maintain good mental health, parenting practices for parents with teens, and healthy ways for teens to cope with anxiety and school issues.

Mila enjoyed her first evening of the radio show. Most of the calls were from youth that wanted advice on how to handle problems with their peers and bullying issues. The calls that had the most impact on Mila were from young ladies who wanted to talk about how they could improve their self-esteem. Mila was passionate about helping teenage girls to build a healthier sense of self-esteem. As her alarm went off, Mila thought "welcome to no more sleeping in on Saturdays!" as the radio show would run every Saturday from 7 a.m. to 10 a.m. in addition to the Friday evening segment. As she complained, Mila felt truly blessed and humbled that God allowed her to receive such an excellent opportunity to further her career. The next few years were sure to be challenging but in the end, it would all pay off.

Upon arriving at the station, Mila thought the station manager was going to be a handful. He had a con artist way of interacting with people that made Mila not totally trust him, but she would handle him the way she handled most things in her life—prayer. The morning at the radio station went by faster than Mila thought it would and she actually ended up enjoying the program and helping all those who called in. She had a lot of work ahead of her to keep the radio show fresh and interesting. Mila's ringing phone brought her out of her daydream.

"Hey Denise." Mila knew that her best friend was checking to see how her first weekend of the radio show went.

"How was the show?" Denise asked.

"It seems like it's going to be a lot of work but both days went very well and the callers weren't too bad," Mila answered. "It will be a challenging year but I'm up for it."

"You'll be fine." Denise stated. "Just take it one show at a time."

"Yeah. I know God is definitely going to be with me through this new endeavor." Mila would definitely need to continue daily talks and prayer with God. "For the next few years my schedule and time will be very tight."

"HaHaHa... Girl, I'm sure you will manage it all just fine. How are you doing with the break up with Brian?"

"Denise, I'm doing fine with it. I do feel bad for Brian now that I know about the tragedy that took place in his childhood. But girl, he's called me several times a day since the breakup."

"Oh... Well, you all were in a relationship for four years so give him some time to adjust."

"I understand that it's hard for him. That's why I answered the first call but I decided that I couldn't answer any more of his calls. It would just make it more difficult to adjust to the breakup."

"Well girl, just make sure you handle it the way you think best."

"Denise, I've made my decision and I know this is best for me and Brian."

Once she and Denise ended their conversation, Mila decided to just chill out after being at the radio station so early in the morning. Sitting in his apartment alone, Brian felt worse than he had when his mother died. He knew he should follow Mila's advice and seek counseling but he just wasn't motivated to deal with this right now. In his mind, Brian wanted to get Mila back first and then he would figure out the counseling thing.

Meanwhile back in the Midwest, Terrence was thinking of Mila and wondering if his heart could handle another relationship. Terrence decided to pray and allow God to direct his decision making. Terrence felt like he did not want to let Mila get away. He just wasn't too sure about this long-distance thing. But he had not met a woman like Mila with whom he could fully share his faith in God. This time he would allow God to direct the relationship.

Terrence still had some healing to do. The realization came when he heard his own voice as he talked about his painful relationship and the devastating way his engagement ended. This was the time when he really needed to continue to attend Bible study and Men's Fellowship and surround himself with other men who were strong in their faith in God. Terrence would continue to give himself the time to heal as he got to know Mila better. Today, he realized that he missed her already and wanted to see her soon.

On the other side of town, Regina was still trying to plot and plan to keep Terrence and Mila apart. She had become a bitter and cruel woman who did not want to see anyone else happy. If Regina carried out her plan, it could prove to be troublesome for Terrence and Mila.

# 17 THE MONTH OF LOVE

"Man, this month has flown by." Mila could not believe that February was about to start. It seemed like January had just gotten underway. Mila's radio show was in full swing and the ratings were higher than expected. January had brought a newness of life for Mila. She and Terrence enjoyed numerous talks over the month that helped them to get to know one another better.

Each week Terrence had sent Mila beautiful bouquets of flowers after he heard her say that she loved having fresh flowers around. The arrangements were more beautiful and elaborate than the next. Mila loved this kind of attention and was enjoying getting to know Terrence. The two had planned for Terrence to come visit Mila for a long weekend over the President's Day Holiday as Mila did not have to work on that Monday.

Their time apart was coming to an end as February had arrived. The two were also getting nervous about spending time together alone and wondered if what they experienced was just a little holiday fling.

"Man, are you ready for your visit with Mila?" Greg asked Terrence.

"Man. It's no sweat. We're just hanging out. No biggie." On the inside Terrence was shaking.

"Okay. Just remember that she is not your ex-fiancé and give her the benefit of the doubt. And by all means try to relax and enjoy yourself."

"HaHaHa.... Dude, I got this. I'm just planning to have an enjoyable weekend and see the sites in the area. I really liked the East Coast when I lived there before and can't wait to visit."

"Man, make sure you have Mila take you to Lauriol Plaza. Their food is the bomb. She took our family there when we came out to visit. The food is a lot better than 'The Place'."

"Oh wow... That is saying a whole lot because you love 'The Place.' Okay. I will put that on my list of places to go."

Friday had finally arrived and Terrence was ready to board his flight to see Mila. Mila was a flurry of nerves. She wanted everything to be perfect for this visit with Terrence. Mila had planned a quiet evening on Friday with a home-cooked meal for Terrence. She heard Terrence say that he loved sweet potato pie so she asked her mother for an easy way to make one. Mila knew the pie had turned out perfectly when the crust bubbled to a beautiful golden color and she could smell the cinnamon and nutmeg. Her apartment smelled wonderful with the aroma of the baking. Mila also cooked a baked salmon filet seasoned with garlic and lemon pepper with a touch of coconut oil, as well as steamed vegetables and baked sweet potatoes. Of course, she had a chilled bottle of white wine and beer for Terrence if he wanted it.

Mila took extra care with her appearance this morning. Her usual Friday attire is jeans and a relaxed shirt with a pair of casual shoes. Today, Mila wore a cute pair of designer boot cut jeans with a pretty V-neck sweater in the richest color of purple. The outfit was topped off with a cute pair of leather boots and of course silver jewelry. Mila's make up was immaculately applied and she had an extra pep in her step today. What Mila did not know was that Terrence thought she was beautiful whether she had makeup on or not. Mila left work a little early to ensure that she was on time picking Terrence up from the airport.

She had not been this nervous since she first left home for the hallowed halls of university life. Deep down she knew that this was going to be a great weekend. Terrence was standing at the loading area near baggage claim when Mila arrived at the airport. He looked absolutely handsome standing there in his Calvin Klein wool coat with matching hat and gloves. Mila loved a well-dressed man. Terrence was impeccably dressed each time that Mila saw him.

Mila hopped out of the car and Terrence swooped her up in his arms in a big warm hug. Mila felt right at home in Terrence's arms. "You ready?" Mila asked Terrence.

"Yes. Let's go. What do you have planned this evening?" Terrence was curious about what this weekend would hold.

"Tonight, I thought we could spend a quiet evening in with a home-cooked meal." Mila was now starting to relax.

"That sounds like a good idea. The flight was a little bumpy and I would like to settle down a bit before you take me out on the town."

"HaHaHa!! Who said I was taking you out on the town?" Mila teased Terrence.

"I did. And I know you are going to show me a great time this weekend." Terrence was really looking forward to spending a fantastic weekend with Mila.

"I'll give you that one Mr. Harper. We will have a great weekend!"

Once at Mila's condo, Terrence unpacked and sat on the bar stool watching Mila finish dinner. "Do you want wine or beer?" Mila asked Terrence.

"Beer would be great. I know you're having wine."

"HaHaHa!! So now you think you know me?" Mila was amused with Terrence trying to predict what he thought she would be drinking.

"Not at all but I know you like a good glass of wine." Terrence had a smile in his voice when he said this.

"Well, you're right. I will most definitely be having a glass of wine."

Throughout dinner, Mila and Terrence had a light banter of flirting going on. They both enjoyed the meal and Terrence was surprised that Mila could cook as well as her mother Linda. After dinner, they moved to the couch in the living area to watch television.

"Dinner was great!" Terrence exclaimed. "I had no idea you could cook almost as well as your mother." He stated with a laugh.

"Thank you. Cooking comes naturally for most women in our family. I primarily cook out of necessity. Baking is what I enjoy. I love to bake and use it to clear my head when I have had a long or difficult day."

Terrence and Mila spent the next several hours watching television and enjoying one another's company. They talked at length about their plans for the future and what they wanted for their lives. Terrence was impressed with the fact that Mila's career was on the fast track with the start of her radio show, which was contributing to the increase of her private practice. This man sitting next to her amazed Mila. He had endured the most embarrassing situation when he was engaged and dumped before they could make it to the altar and to hear him speak about his faith in God after that ordeal was remarkable. Both would enjoy getting to know one another one day at a time.

Meanwhile, back in Michigan, Regina was up to her old tricks. She was furious that Terrence decided to go visit Mila for the weekend. It had been easy to get the information. One of the secretaries in Terrence's office in New York was friends with Regina and did not know the truth about why she and Terrence broke up. This secretary listened in on a conversation that Terrence's secretary was having with him about his schedule for the week. When Regina spoke to the secretary, she told her everything about the upcoming trip to visit Mila.

Regina stood in her living room trying to figure out what she would do next. Regina really did not have any idea what she was up against. She did not know where Mila lived or how she lived. Regina was about to change all of that. She begged, borrowed, and schemed to get the money to fly to the metropolitan Washington, DC area where Mila lived. But how would she find out Mila's address?

Regina was a sick and desperate woman. Until she received treatment for her mental health issues she would continue to display this dangerous, paranoid behavior. After mulling it over in her head, Regina decided to hide in the bushes of Linda Warrington's home until she was sure no one would see her. Once she felt that the street was quiet and no one was watching, Regina looked in Linda's mailbox to see if there was anything in there from Mila. To her pleased surprise, Regina found a letter with Mila's return address on it. "Washington, DC, here I come!" Regina shouted with evil in her voice.

As Terrence and Mila were enjoying their quiet evening at Mila's condo, they had no idea that Regina was spying on them from outside the locked balcony. Because the blinds were drawn she could only catch glimpses of them. She had decided to sleep in her car that night so that she could catch them leaving the apartment the next day. Regina was bound and determined to get her ex-fiancé back, resorting to drastic measures if called for.

The next day, Mila and Terrence started out early for a full day of sightseeing. Mila took Terrence to one of the Smithsonian's to view an exhibit on African-American life in America. From there they went on a special tour of the White House that Mila arranged through a friend that worked for a senator. From there they went to the Blacks in Wax Museum in Maryland. This was one of the best times Terrence has had and he could not believe that Mila was living in a place that housed the rich history of America.

For lunch, they took Greg's advice and headed to Lauriol Plaza for the best Latin food in the area. Terrence couldn't believe that he was having such a great time. He hated to see the weekend end and started thinking about what it would be like to spend the rest of his life with Mila. Terrence realized that he was moving way ahead of himself but he had never felt this way before and did not want to waste another day without Mila in his life.

Mila was having a great time, too. She really enjoyed her time with Terrence and was looking forward to the rest of the weekend. Mila did not know what the future would hold but wanted to see where things would go with Terrence. Although she was having a fantastic weekend, Mila had an uncomfortable feeling. She could have sworn that someone was following them. Each time she turned around to look, though, no one was there.

"This has been one of the best weekends I've had in a long time," Terrence shared with Mila as they were having lunch.

"I'm glad that you're having a good time. I wanted to make sure that everything was perfect on your first visit."

"Well, you succeeded. I'm having a truly great time. But I must admit, I'm wondering how all of this is going to work out with us living in different places." Terrence was starting to let the doubt creep in.

"I don't know." Mila was starting to get worried. "I figured we would just take things one day at a time and figure it out as we went along."

"Okay. But how will we nurture a relationship long distance? Long distance relationships can be challenging." Terrence was letting it all out now.

"I know that you have had some challenges in the past but you can't let that impact our relationship." Mila was trying not to over analyze this. "I'm not your ex-fiancé and you have to give me the benefit of the doubt or this will not work."

Sitting in the booth behind Mila and Terrence, Regina could hear their entire conversation. A smile formed on her face when she heard that what she had done to Terrence was still impacting him. In her twisted mind, she thought that meant he still had feelings for her. The opposite couldn't be more true.

Terrence and Mila continued their conversation finally deciding that they would alternate the months that they would visit one another. They also had to be mindful of Mila's schedule at the radio station. They were faithful that it would all work out the way that God intended it to. For now, however, Mila and Terrence only had two more days to go on their visit so they decided to make the most of their time together.

Since they had missed spending Valentine's Day together, Terrence had a special surprise for Mila once they returned to her apartment. After they got settled in, Mila heard a knock on the door. When she opened the door, the deliveryman was standing there holding the most exquisite bouquet of two-dozen white roses with a single pink rose in the middle.

"Oh my gosh, these are beautiful," Mila exclaimed in a loud voice causing Terrence to run to the room where Mila was standing to see what was going on. When she turned around and saw him standing there, Mila gave Terrence the biggest most sensual kiss on the lips.

"I take it you like the flowers." Terrence asked with a smile on his face.

"They are so beautiful." Mila was smiling now.

"Well, I have one more surprise," Terrence stated as he pulled a beautiful velvet box from behind his back.

"What's this?" Mila could not handle one more surprise. She opened the box to see the most beautiful platinum and diamond open-heart necklace. "Terrence, you didn't have to get me a gift. But, Thank you." Mila exclaimed while admiring the necklace.

"I saw the necklace and was hoping that when you wear it you would think of me and open your heart to the possibility of a new beginning with me."

Mila was speechless. Instead of saying something she gave Terrence another kiss. On Sunday, Terrence and Mila spent the first part of the day at church and then went to brunch at the Four Season's. This was one of Terrence's favorite places to have brunch. He reminisced about his days in New York going to places like this for brunch. During brunch, they reflected on the sermon from that morning and felt more committed to ensuring that they were living their lives in service to God.

They continued to talk about their budding relationship and their plans for the next visit. After brunch, they spent a few hours strolling down Wisconsin Avenue in Georgetown stopping to browse in a few shops along the way. As they were leaving a popular cupcake spot, Brian bumped into the couple.

Mila looked up and saw Brian with hurt and betrayal in his eyes. "Hello Brian."

Brian was cut so deep at seeing Mila with another man that he almost couldn't speak. "Hello Mila. I see that you wasted no time in moving on." Cutting his eyes in Terrence's direction.

"Brian, don't do this. Things were over between us long before we decided to officially breakup." Mila noticed that Terrence had stepped a little closer to her. "Brian, this is Terrence."

The two men didn't say anything. Terrence went to extend his hand to Brian but noticed that Brian had quickly turned around and started walking away.

"I can't believe that she is already with someone else. I never should've told her about my mother and family. I just should've found a way to fix things with Mila. I'm not letting her get away that easy." Brian was deep in thought and felt the cut in his heart getting deeper.

After spying on them last night, Regina had decided she would chill in her hotel room and prepare for her flight home the next day. In her confused mind, she thought she still somehow had a chance to get Terrence back.

Back at Mila's condo, "Terrence, I'm sorry about that. I guess Brian is having a more difficult time adjusting to the breakup than I thought."

"Mila you don't have anything to apologize for. Hey, I can understand where he is coming from. If I had just lost a woman as wonderful as you I would react the same way."

"Thank you for being so understanding Terrence and you're pretty wonderful yourself." Mila was hoping Brian would not cause any problems for she and Terrence.

"You know, the weekend goes by too fast," Mila was saying to Terrence as she prepared to take him to the airport on Monday morning.

"I agree. I'm definitely not ready to leave." Terrence was missing Mila already. "What if I moved here so that we could get our relationship off to a strong start?"

Mila was not sure how she felt about that. Things were starting to move very fast now. "You mean in your own place?" Mila asked. She did not believe in living with any man before she was married.

"Of course," Terrence said. "I know that you don't want to live with anyone before marriage. I can come back in April to look for a place and then we can visit together again."

"Okay. That sounds like a plan." Uncertainty was in Mila's voice.

As they pulled up to the airport, they had finalized their plans for

Terrence's move to Washington, DC, by May.

# 18 BITTER

"I'm so glad to be home."  Regina hated flying and was glad that the plane landed at the airport without any problems. Regina had become such a vindictive and mean spirited woman.  Her trip to spy on Mila and Terrence only added fuel to that mean spiritedness. Regina's new mission this year would be to destroy any happiness Mila and Terrence thought they would have.  In that moment, Regina realized that she did not want Terrence back she just did not want to see him happy and was going to cause as many problems for him and Mila as she could. If she could not be happy then she was going to make everyone around her miserable.

Regina did not recognize that God was in control and it was He that would have the last say. Regina had forgotten about her upbringing in the church and the values that were instilled in her at Sunday school and the other youth meetings at the church.  She had not prayed or gone to church in such a long time that all the love and goodness had left her. Regina allowed it to be replaced with hatred, anger, and the worst kind of evil.

Not only had Regina stopped going to church and believing in God, she stopped taking her medication to treat symptoms of bipolar disorder and had cut off all contact with her therapist.  She threw aside any recollection of her family history with mental illness and how it had damaged all their relationships.

With so many family members not receiving treatment for their mental health issues, including her mother, Regina never received all the love and care that she needed as a child and her insecurities and feelings of inferiority increased. This left her feeling empty and alone, which further made it difficult for her to accept love from another person or give love in return.

"If it is the last thing I do I'm going to destroy whatever relationship Mila and Terrence are planning to have." Regina took a shot of liquor as devious and cruel thoughts entered her head.

# 19 VISIT HOME

Time was moving swiftly along for Mila. The first couple of months of her radio show were going much better than anyone expected. Mila was catching on quickly to the radio business and had developed a great working relationship with her producer. The calls were becoming more challenging with the types of problems that were reported, from incest to self-injurious behaviors, but Mila loved a good challenge and wanted to do all she could as a mental health professional to help those in need. She wished those in the African-American community really understood the value of therapy and seeking professional help for mental health issues.

The month of March was coming in like a soft kitten. The weather was beautiful. The cold wintry weather was now starting to be replaced with sunny skies and the first smell of spring. The color was starting to come back to Earth with flowers springing up and leaves growing back on trees. There was warmth in the air that smelled of a fresh sweetness to let you know that new beginnings were on their way.

Speaking of new beginnings, it seems that things are working in Mila and Terrence's favor. Terrence's company is opening a new office in the metropolitan Washington, DC, area so Terrence's move was coming right on time. Terrence's new office would be in the heart of downtown DC but he would still be able to work from home as he had done the last few years. At least now, if he needed to go into the office it would be a car ride or metro stop away.

Mila would be traveling to the Midwest in a few days to surprise her family and hang out with her cousins. She and Terrence would also talk about his move to DC and the areas he should consider in his search for a new home.

Mila's phone rang interrupting her thoughts. "Hello." Mila answered.

"Hey girl."

"What's up? I was just heading out." Mila stated.

"Nothing." Her cousin Desiree answered. "Where are you headed?"

"I have a meeting with my producer," Mila said.

"Okay. Don't panic but Granny had to be taken to the hospital. She is stable but you know your mom is stressing."

"What happened?" Mila was very worried about her grandmother and mother.

"She became a little light-headed and passed out." Desiree knew her cousin was worrying but their family is so close knit that their grandmother is being supported very well.

"I've never known granny to get light-headed."

"The doctors think that she had a vitamin deficiency. She may have to change her diet. They're going to keep her in the hospital for a few more days." Desiree hoped this information would reassure her cousin about their grandmother's health.

"So, things are going to be okay with granny?" Mila blew out a big breath.

"Yes, the doctor just wants to monitor her for a few days in the hospital."

"Okay. I'm sure God has granny covered." Mila would definitely say a prayer for her grandmother. "By the way Desi, has anyone heard from Tim?"

"No. This is the longest that he has been gone and granny is over the top with worry. We think that is part of what is going on with her right now."

"Oh my... Has anyone called the police to file a missing persons' report?"

"Yes. Uncle Brad called them at the end of February and filed a missing persons' report. He also talked to a friend who has some connection with Veterans' Affairs in case Tim ended up at one of the hospitals."

"Good. I sure hope Tim shows up soon. Ooh, Desi, I'll have to call you back I have to leave the house now before I'm late for my appointment." Mila was so glad she had decided a while ago to go home and surprise her family.

"Heavenly Father, I thank you first for my family and the love that you have given to us to share. I thank you for my grandmother and the life you have given to her. I ask Lord that you would send your word out over my grandmother and heal her. Your word says that by your stripes we are healed. Father, I also want to ask you to watch over and protect my cousin Tim. Please keep him safe and bring him back home to us soon. I thank you in advance for hearing and answering all my prayers. In the precious name of Jesus, I pray. Amen." Mila felt renewed and confident that God would take care of her grandmother and Tim.

Friday came and Mila prepared to board her flight to her Midwestern hometown. As much as she loved to travel, Mila hated airports. There were always so many lines and angry people. The workers at the airlines never seemed to have any information and TSA had been taking their jobs way too seriously since 9/11. Today, Mila must definitely be experiencing God's favor. The line in security was short and Mila made it to her gate with thirty minutes to spare and collect herself before boarding her flight.

The flight to Michigan was relatively short and Mila was thankful for that. She was anxious to see her granny and mother especially since she knew her granny had been in the hospital and was still being monitored closely. She was also excited about seeing Terrence since they had not seen each other since February. The added benefit was that she would also get to hang out with her cousins.

Terrence had been spoiling Mila since he left in February. The gifts had been pouring in. Not only was Terrence still sending Mila the weekly flower arrangements, he sent her diamond earrings one week to match the necklace he gave her in February. A few weeks ago Terrence made arrangements with the spa Mila frequented in Maryland, to give her a full day of spa services. Mila got a one-hour massage, facial, and spa manicure and pedicure. She thoroughly enjoyed the day and planned to give Terrence a big "Thank You" for that one.

Not only was Terrence thoughtful but he was also paying attention to the things she shared with him that she liked. That definitely gave him some points with Mila. Mila had an uneventful flight and was happy to land. She picked up her rental car and headed towards her hometown. Mila loved driving on the highway. It allowed her time to think and clear her head before the next activity.

Mila pulled up to her mother's home and was greeted by the smell of her favorite cake baking in the oven. Mila surprising her mother, greeted her with a big, warm hug and went to the den where her granny was resting to greet her with a kiss as well. Mila left her granny resting and prepared to call Desiree so that they could finalize their plans for the evening. She and Desiree decided that the cousins would come over to the Warrington home and they would order pizza tonight and plan a big night out later this weekend since Mila would be in town until Wednesday.

Mila decided to freshen up and change into yoga pants and a t-shirt for this relaxing evening in with her cousins. While Mila waited for Desiree and the rest of their cousins to arrive, Terrence surprised her by showing up to the Warrington home. Mila greeted Terrence with a sensual kiss. Terrence was so thoughtful in bringing flowers for her mother and grandmother. He was so happy to see Mila he could not contain himself.

He marveled at how beautiful this woman was and how much he could see God working in her life. Terrence shared with Mila that he planned to look for a condo in the city not too far from the new office his company was opening. In April, he would check out the condos the real estate agent hired by his company recommended. Terrence also told

Mila he had a special surprise for her on her trip home that she would get later. The new couple talked and enjoyed one another's company until the other Warrington grandchildren arrived.

"Hey Mila!" Her cousins bellowed.

"I thought this was going to be just the cousins hanging out?" Desiree asked as she noticed Terrence sitting next to Mila and being a little possessive of the time the cousins would share this evening. The other cousins went straight to the den to check in on their granny.

"I'm leaving," Terrence chuckled as he got up to get his coat and head for the door. He gave Mila a quick kiss on the cheek and said good-bye to the rest of the Warrington clan in the house.

"What happened to 'we are taking it one day at a time'?" Desiree teased her cousin.

"We are taking it one day at a time," Mila responded defensively. "I didn't know Terrence was stopping by. He decided to surprise me before you guys came over."

The cousins continued talking and watching movies while checking in on their grandmother. Mila and her cousins decided to order pizza from their favorite place and shared wine that evening. Satisfied that their grandmother was feeling good and resting well, the cousins headed into the basement to continue eating, drinking wine, and watching movies. They joked and laughed with one another until the wee hours of the morning.

Their family was very strong in their faith and knew that their grandmother would be back up and feeling like her old self soon. The cousins all agreed to attend church together on Sunday and be more committed to their relationship with God. These cousins were growing in their relationship with one another and vowed from that day forward to ensure that the rich legacy of their family would continue.

# 20 ROMANTIC DINNER

The next morning Mila and her family decided to meet for breakfast. They filled the little café with a flurry of activity as their plates of pancakes, eggs, hash browns, bacon, and coffee were passed from the waitress. The family engaged in their usual loud talking and boisterous familial interactions. Mila's aunts and uncles were surprised that she came to visit but were glad to have their niece home. The family talked with one another for several hours at the little café before heading out to run their usual Saturday errands.

Mila went back to her mother's house to chill for a bit before her night out with Terrence. She loved her family and always enjoyed hanging out with them but had decided that she was going to escape from them for a little bit this evening. Mila and her cousins had decided that they would all attend church together on Sunday morning to strengthen their bond as family and give thanks to God for his many wonderful blessings.

Once back at Linda's home, Mila decided instead of chilling, she would do some research and reading for her next radio show. "This is the driest reading!" Mila exclaimed out loud. As Mila read, her eyes became heavy and she dozed off for a bit.

Mila was awakened by a loud thud at the big bay window in the living room. "What in the world is going on?" Mila asked, confused as she ran to the window to see what happened. Upon reaching the window, Mila thought she saw a figure running down the street that had a strong resemblance to Regina.

Barely making it to her parked car and completely out of breath, Regina ducked down in the front seat so no one would see her. "Oh shoot! That was close. I'm going to find out why that little witch has come back to town this weekend. I must do better with my spying so that I don't get caught. I have to quickly get my plan underway because I'm tired of all of this following Mila around."

Once she was sure that no one was lurking around outside of her mother's home, Mila went upstairs to get ready for her date with Terrence. He asked Mila to accompany him to dinner with some work associates who were in town on business and had brought their wives with them. Mila was a little shocked that Terrence wanted her to meet his colleagues but she agreed.

Mila decided to wear a simple, black, sheath dress with a single strand pearl necklace and of course four-inch stilettos. Her makeup was very simple this evening with more natural colors and pink lip gloss on her lips. Audrey Hepburn inspired her attire for the evening from the movie Breakfast at Tiffany's. Mila looked very elegant. The weather was very nice for this time of the year so Mila was able to wear a lightweight trench coat.

As Mila descended the stairs, Terrence was waiting for her at the bottom of the staircase in a trance.

"You look very beautiful this evening." Terrence liked that Mila looked as if she was not wearing a lot of makeup and it showed the true beauty of her skin.

"Thank you Mr. Harper. You look very handsome this evening." And Terrence did look like he just stepped off the cover of GQ magazine. Mila was a sucker for a black man dressed in a well-tailored suit.

Terrence helped Mila out of the door and made sure she was settled comfortably in the passenger side of the car. The couple drove to the only 5-star, reservations only restaurant in their hometown listening to the sounds of jazz playing in the car.

"Ms. Warrington, what are you trying to do to me this evening?" Terrence asked with a twinkle in his eye.

"Why Mr. Harper I don't think I know what you're talking about." Mila responded with mischief in her voice.

"You don't do you. You have on this amazing black dress that is hugging your curves in all the right places, your face looks fresh like it has a natural glow, and you smell exotic and sweet." Terrence's attraction to Mila was growing each day.

"Thank you Terrence. I could say the same for you. You surprised me with the most beautiful cocktail ring this evening, you look amazing in your tailor-made suit, and ever since I told you that purple was one of my favorite colors you've been wearing little touches of it whenever I see you." Mila thought Terrence was one of the most well dressed men she had met.

"HaHaHa... How very perceptive of you. I like to pay attention to the details and since I plan on spending a lot of time with you, I want that time to be enjoyable for both of us so I'm paying attention to all of the things you like."

"I like a man who knows what to pay attention to." Mila felt like Terrence was truly interested in developing a lasting relationship with her.

The couple continued to the restaurant enjoying being in each other's company and listening to jazz playing on the CD player. Once they arrived to the restaurant, Terrence had the valet park the car and he ushered Mila inside. Mila and Terrence arrived a little early so that they could enjoy some time alone before the other couples arrived. Mila thought this restaurant was beautiful. From their seat on the rotating top level, Mila and Terrence had an amazing view of the clear blue night with stars twinkling in the sky.

While waiting for the other couples to arrive, Mila ordered a glass of champagne and Terrence ordered bourbon on the rocks.

"I just knew you were going to order a beer. I don't think I have ever seen you order liquor before." Mila stated.

"I don't usually but on occasion I like a good bourbon and I know this place has a high-end brand."

Once their drinks arrived, Terrence and Mila continued to just relax and enjoy each other's company. Mila was enjoying being in Terrence's company and did a little flirting. She slightly ran the tip of her foot over his legs as she was sitting close to him. Terrence was taking in the sweet smell of her perfume and was enjoying the touches from Mila. Just as Terrence was about to embrace Mila the other couples arrived.

Mila soon found that Terrence's colleagues had wives who were just as accomplished and successful as their husbands. These women were at the top of their fields in various professions from medicine to government agencies and they seemed to be genuinely interested in Mila's new professional endeavor. The couples enjoyed great conversations and vowed to continue these dinner dates with one another once Terrence moved to Washington, DC.

The managers in the new office that Terrence would be opening were excited about the new changes taking place in their company and the fresh ideas that Terrence would be bringing as their new boss. It was an exciting time for them and they could not wait to see how their company would grow under Terrence's leadership.

The couples said their good-byes and headed to their respective cars. Once inside Terrence's car, Mila asked, "So what was this evening really about?"

"These are the men I will be working closely with and we will frequently be socializing with them and their wives. Since they were in town I thought it would be good to get together with them for dinner." Terrence also wanted to see how Mila would interact with the wives, as he knew this was an issue for Regina in their relationship.

"So do you think that these managers will be open to you as their new boss?"

"I think we will all work well together. I know it will be an adjustment but I believe that all the men present are team players and are ready to take the company to the next level. What did you think of their wives?"

"I thought their wives were very accomplished, intelligent women in their own right and I spent a lot of the evening wondering how they juggled their own successful careers with supporting their husbands."

"What conclusion did you come up with? Do you think with all that you have accomplished in your education and career that you will be able to submit as a wife?"

"I honestly don't know. Sometimes when I think of the word *submit* it has such a negative connotation to it. I do know that as long as my husband is submitted to Christ then I won't have a problem submitting to him. This is an area I struggle with because I am so independent and have been the sole provider for myself for so long. I know that I will have to really study my Bible and look at examples of Godly wives in scripture to guide me as a wife." Mila hoped she was giving Terrence the answer he was looking for.

Terrence was thinking that was not the answer he was looking for but sensed that Mila had been honest and transparent in her response. "Did you find my co-workers stuffy or boring?"

"Not at all. I had a really great time and can't wait to socialize with all of them once you move to the area." Mila knew that Terrence asked this question based on Regina's actions in their relationship. If this was going to work Terrence had to leave the past in the past and realize that she was not his ex-fiancé.

They arrived at Linda's home and Terrence walked Mila to the door. At the door, Terrence grabbed Mila in a passionate embrace before getting back in his car and heading home.

Once inside the house, Mila thought that she really did not know if she answered the question about submitting to Terrence's satisfaction, but she had answered it honestly. Mila knew that the women of her grandmothers' generation submitted to their husbands in the traditional sense of the word. Her grandfather was the true patriarch and head of household of their family. Her grandmother, Mrs. Warrington, submitted to her husband in every sense of the word as a wife is supposed to. Mila knew she and the women of her generation had a different sense of submitting with all the achievements they had accomplished in their education and careers. No longer did women just stay home, they were running corporations and were also in high positions in the political arena. But Mila knew that she wanted a marriage like her grandparents had so she would consult God about her view of submitting to her husband.

Sitting in his living room, Terrence wondered if Mila would be able to submit to him as his wife. Would she be able to support him while juggling the demands of her career and growing private practice as well as with the added demands on her schedule with the radio show?

Terrence knew that Mila had given him her honest answer but after his last failed relationship and broken engagement, Terrence knew that he wanted to marry a woman who knew exactly what it meant to be a wife and committed to the relationship. Terrence would pray about this and seek God's guidance. One thing for sure, he was not going to stop seeing Mila. She was the woman he had been waiting for all his life.

# 21 THE FAMILY THAT PRAYS TOGETHER

The next day Mila and her cousins attended church with their grandmother as promised. The elder Mrs. Warrington was doing much better and had started to gain her strength back. As usual Mila's family filled up one side of the church. The service was truly spirit-filled. The pastor talked a lot about God's love and how we should show our love for God by loving one another. Family was a central focus of the sermon and reminded Mila and her cousins about their commitment to their family.

After service, Mila and her family headed to dinner at Red Lobster. This was not Mila's first choice of a restaurant for dinner but she knew that her grandmother and mother really liked to come here after church on Sunday. Mila's family filled up an entire area of the restaurant. They were a swirl of activity and talking as they all reflected on the sermon from church this morning.

"Girl how was your date last night?" Desiree whispered to her cousin so no one else would hear.

"Fantastic! We had the most amazing evening! I will have to tell you more later," Mila responded.

"What are you all down there whispering about?" asked Mila's

Aunt Brenda.

"They're probably talking about Mila's date last night with Terrence," remarked Mila's Aunt Joyce.

Mila and Desiree looked at one another with confusion as if to ask how their Aunt Joyce knew about her date with Terrence.

Aunt Joyce reading the looks on their faces offered an explanation on how she knew about the date. "One of my friends has a daughter that was working at the restaurant last night and saw you and Terrence having dinner with some other couples. She called and asked me if you and Terrence were dating."

"Does everyone in this town always end up at the same place at the same time?" Mila thought as her Aunt Joyce was talking.

"I told her that I didn't know anything about Mila and Terrence dating. So, Mila what exactly is going on between you and Terrence?" Aunt Joyce could be very nosy at times.

Sensing her granddaughter's discomfort and knowing how private she is, the elder Mrs. Warrington steered the conversation in a different direction. "So Mila, how is that big-headed cousin Brandon of yours doing at school?" Ms. Warrington felt more at ease about her grandson being away from home since he decided to go to a college near where Mila lived.

As Mila answered, she thought, thank God for grandmothers as she was grateful that her grandmother changed the topic of the conversation. She did not want to discuss her relationship with Terrence in front of all her family. "Granny he is doing well. We don't get to see each other or talk as often due to our hectic schedules but we make it a point to at least have some kind of contact on a monthly basis."

"Okay. Don't let your schedules get in the way of maintaining a healthy relationship with your family. You and Brandon have to support one another since you two are the only family you have in that area." Mrs. Warrington's thoughts went to her grandson, Tim who no one had heard from in months. She hoped the police would have some news for them soon.

"Yes ma'am," Mila responded, knowing better than to dispute anything her grandmother said.

After finishing their meal and greeting various neighbors that entered the restaurant, the Warrington clan left in the same flurry of activity with which they had entered the restaurant. Mila's aunts and uncles hugged and kissed their niece and wished her safe travels back to her home.

Once back at her mother's house, Mila's mother and grandmother both went to their respective rooms to rest a little while. Mila took this opportunity to peacefully watch some old black and white movies on the classic movie channel. She was pleasantly surprised to see that the featured movie today was *Mahogany* instead of the usual black and white movies from the early 1940s. Mila settled into the comfy big chair in the living room and watched one of her favorite classic movies. She loved the fashion scene in Italy and the love story that was unfolding between the characters played by Diana Ross and Billie Dee Williams.

The buzzing of Mila's phone interrupted her quiet afternoon.

"Hello beautiful." Terrence's voice was dripping with honey and Mila loved when he called her beautiful.

"Well hello to you to. How was your Sunday?" Mila had a huge smile in her voice.

"It was good. Church was on fire this morning and I treated the folks to dinner after church. What about you?"

"The same. The whole Warrington Clan went to church this morning and then all of us went to dinner afterwards. You can imagine the chaos that ensued." Mila loved her family but it could be an ordeal when they all decided to go out to eat together or any other group activity.

"HaHaHa... I can only imagine. I'm sure it was a big ball of activity." Terrence knew firsthand how much activity took place in the

Warrington family when they were together as he witnessed through his friendship with Greg.

"Oh and get this. My Aunt Joyce started asking me questions about you and I. A daughter of one of her friends saw us out at dinner last night and asked Aunt Joyce if you and I were dating."

"Are you serious? This town can be so small sometimes." Terrence was curious about how Mila answered the question. "What did you say?"

"I didn't say anything. Granny changed the topic of the conversation." Mila was still thankful for that smooth move by her grandmother.

"How would you have answered?" Terrence was feeling a little unsettled.

"I'm not sure. I'm a very private person and there are some things that I only talk about with certain people." Mila knew that since she listened to other people's problems for a living, she sometimes found it hard to talk about herself or her problems. "Also, the last time we talked we said we would be taking things one day at a time. We have not really said where we are going with this relationship." Mila did not want to rush things especially since the breakup with Brian was only a few months old.

"You are correct. But Mila you have to know that I care about you deeply and you are the only woman that I want to spend time with. I have a strong attraction to you and I am not about to let you go now that we have found one another." Terrence was putting everything on the line and feeling a little nervous about having such strong feelings for Mila. He really had not felt this way about a woman since his tragic breakup.

"Thank you for letting me know that. I wasn't sure how you felt, especially after last night and my answer to your question about submitting. I care about you a lot as well and you're the only man I'm interested in dating. But after Brian I'm not wasting a bunch of years dating another man just to have it go nowhere, to not move towards a strong commitment."

"Thank you for being honest. Your answer was not what I was looking for but I know you gave me an honest and sincere answer. Trust me, Mila. I'm not looking to waste your time. At this age and time in my life, I'm looking for a committed relationship with the woman that God has chosen for me. I believe you are that woman. When I move to the DC area in April we can continue this discussion." Terrence's feelings for Mila were so strong that they scared him.

"Fair enough. I can't wait for you to move and for us to continue taking things one day at a time with this relationship." Mila feared being hurt again and was doing all she could to protect her heart from another disappointment.

"The real reason I called was to see if you would have dinner with me at my place on Tuesday evening?"

"I would love to. Consider it a date." Mila couldn't wait to see how Terrence lived and how his house would be decorated. "

Great! I will touch base early on Tuesday so that we can firm up the time." Terrence loved spending time with Mila and couldn't wait to have her visit him at his home.

With the conversation ended, Mila continued to watch the classic movie channel as her heart did a little flutter at the prospect of a new beginning with Terrence. The whirlwind was beginning to get more intense....

# 22 GIRL TALK

Mila was enjoying a relaxing and rejuvenating visit with her family. The last few months had been so hectic with the radio show and increased clients at her private practice that Mila welcomed this respite with her family and friends. Not to mention that ever since Brian saw Terrence and Mila together back in February he had been leaving her multiple voicemail messages almost every day. It had gotten so bad that Mila had to have his number blocked. Mila decided to surprise her good friend Denise with lunch. She picked up some sandwiches and chips from Subway and headed over to the administration building where Denise's office as superintendent was located.

"Hey Mila. " Denise was surprised to see her friend.

"Hey girl. I know when you get caught up with work you forget to eat so I thought if you had a few minutes to spare we could eat lunch in your office." Mila hadn't been able to spend much time with her friend and missed their long talks.

"Thank you so much. You know I forgot my lunch and things have been so busy that I didn't have time to go out and grab something to eat." Denise was so appreciative of her friend's thoughtfulness.

The two friends went into Denise's office and enjoyed a friendly chat over lunch.

"How has your visit been?" Denise was also concerned about Mila's grandmother.

"The visit has been good. Granny is doing much better and actually following doctor's orders. She and my mom have realized that they have to start making some small changes in their diets and get out to walk and exercise a little more." Mila was more comfortable with the state of her grandmother's health than when she first arrived in town. "How is your day going?"

"Busy. Busy. And more busy." Denise offered while laughing, knowing that she would not want it any other way. "Now tell me the real reason you came with lunch."

"HaHaHa... I can't surprise my good friend with lunch without being accused of having ulterior motives?" Mila knew Denise knew her a lot better than that.

"Girl, please. I know you better than that. And you have that 'I'm freaking out look' on your face."

Mila's face always told exactly what she was thinking. "Girl, I think this thing with Terrence is starting to spiral fast. Yesterday we had a conversation and he told me that I'm the only woman he wants to spend time with and that basically he is already thinking about a commitment and he knows that I am the woman God chose for him."

"Okay. So, what's the problem?" Denise knew her friend could sometimes put walls up and shut down as a way to protect herself.

"There is no problem, per se. I'm not sure if I'm ready for all of that with the break up with Brian being just a few months ago."

"Mila as your friend, I'm telling you to just relax and go with the flow. I know you like Terrence and I know that things between you and Brian have been over longer than just a few months ago. Just enjoy getting to know Terrence and be open to wherever it leads you. He is the one that is lucky that you have decided to allow him to be a part of your life. Don't look for a problem where there is none."

"Okay." Mila appreciated that Denise had a way of putting things in proper perspective. "Girl, thank you. I needed that reminder. I spend so much time helping others deal with their problems that I don't always process my own stuff in a good way. You're right. I'm going to, for once, just go with the flow and not over analyze things."

The two friends finished their lunch and Mila decided to head to the beach so that she could think and write.

# 23 HAPPY HOUR

Mila thought Lake Michigan was the most beautiful body of water and it was right at her back door growing up. Mila loved to come to the beach for peace and tranquility and to just think when she needed to clear her head. Today, the sun shone right off the water casting a perfect glow. Usually, being at the lake relaxed Mila and brought a sense of calmness. But not today, Mila could have sworn someone was following her all day. It started when she went to visit Denise for lunch and even now she had the eerie feeling that someone was watching her.

Mila was right. As she was sitting in her car with her journal in hand preparing to write, Regina was sitting a few cars down watching Mila. Regina still could not figure out why Mila was in town and would not stop until she made everyone around her feel wretched.

As Mila was looking around scoping out the area, she felt her cell phone vibrate.

"Hey Mila. Are you okay?" Terrence had worry in his voice.

"Yea. I'm fine. Why do you ask?"

"I called you a few times and didn't get an answer. That is not usually like you." Terrence did not want to tell Mila that he had a sinking feeling that Regina was following her. Terrence thought so the night he and Mila went to dinner with his co-workers, when he could have sworn he saw Regina's car pulling in the restaurant entrance behind them. Then today, he received this strange video on his cell phone from a phone number he did not recognize. The video was of Mila sitting out at the lake in her car.

"My phone is down inside of my purse and I didn't feel it vibrate. I had lunch with Denise at her job and then I came out to the lake to do some writing and just sit and think." Mila did not like the feeling of having to answer to anyone and thought this phone conversation was very strange as it was not Terrence's usual behavior.

"Okay. Be careful. I'm working late tonight to continue to work on planning for my move. Call me when you leave to meet up with your cousins."

"Sure. Enjoy the rest of your day." After Terrence's strange phone call, Mila decided to call it a day at the lake and head back to her mother's home.

Regina grew bored of following Mila and decided she had enough spying while Mila was on the phone with Terrence.

Mila made it back to her mother's house without incident and decided to take a nap before meeting up with her cousins. Mila had not had this much time to just rest and nap in quite some time and it felt good. She stretched out on her favorite couch in the living room and drifted off to sleep. She had a fitful sleep as thoughts of a committed relationship with Terrence and his move to DC occupied her mind.

"Mila, is everything alright with you?" Linda asked as Mila woke from a very fitful sleep.

"Why does everyone keep asking me if I'm okay today?" Mila was starting to get annoyed. "Yes, I'm fine."

"You were tossing and turning in your sleep and didn't seem to be getting any rest." Linda as usual was concerned about her daughter.

"I'm sorry mom if I sounded annoyed. I have a lot on my plate right now with the private practice growing and the demands of the radio show. I want to be successful at everything I do."

"Mila, don't put so much pressure on yourself. You are a successful young woman and have made your family proud. Is it just work or things with Terrence?"

Shaking her head, Mila replied, "No mom. Its just work. Terrence and I are fine."

"Okay. Just remember, you don't have to rush into anything. Take your time and let God direct you."

"I will mom. Now, I'm going to get dressed and meet up with Desiree, Renee, and Ryan."

"I'm so glad to see that you and your cousins are close. It reminds me of how my brothers and sisters and I grew up spending time together and making our family bond stronger. Tell the girls I said 'Hi'."

"I will mom." Mila left to go upstairs and dress to meet up with her cousins.

Mila decided on a casual pair of jeans, a pink sweater, ballet flats, and her wool coat as the weather turned very cool on this evening. The cousins decided to meet for happy hour since Mila was leaving on Wednesday.

As usual, Renee and Ryan were late.

"I wish our road dawgs were here," Desiree commented.

"I know. Too bad Brandon had exams and Leigh couldn't get away from work. We would have had so much fun with them. I'm trying to make sure I have a good relationship with all of the cousins so it doesn't seem like we are showing favorites." Mila loved all her cousins but she, Desiree, Brandon, and Leigh clicked with no problems between them.

Renee and Ryan could be a bit much at times and were so different from the other four. Where the other four were more career-focused, Renee and Ryan were focused on the latest town gossip and clubbing. When the cousins were ready for a night out on the town, they knew they could call Renee and Ryan for the best spots to hang out. Even with their differences, the cousins all loved one another and were "ride or die" to the end for the family.

"Hey cousins!" Renee and Ryan greeted in unison.

"Hey ya'll!" Lynn and Desiree greeted as they hugged their cousins.

"Mila, how does it feel to be the talk of the town?" Ryan could not wait to dish dirt with her cousin.

"I'm sure I don't know what you are talking about. Why would I be the talk of this town or any town?" Mila hated being the center of attention. As she answered her cousin, Mila noticed that Ryan seemed to be wearing a lot of makeup. Usually she barely wore any makeup as she had extremely beautiful and sensitive skin. She would ask Ryan about this later.

"Before we start with all of that let's order so we can take advantage of the happy hour prices." Desiree knew when they started talking it would delay them ordering.

The cousins decided to order a bunch of different foods. They had hot wings, spinach and artichoke dip, veggie pizza, chips and salsa, french fries, and mozzarella sticks. They took advantage of the happy hour wines and cocktails. Mila would get back on her eating plan when she returned home. Today she was just going to enjoy hanging out with her cousins.

"Now back to you being the talk of the town." Renee picked up for Ryan.

"Once again why am I the talk of the town? Mila asked.

"Now Mila you know we live in a small town. And Terrence is considered to be a very eligible bachelor that a lot of women in this town tried to get their hooks into. You breeze into town over the holiday and without any effort you have the man eating out of the palm of your hand." Desiree stated all this in a matter of fact tone.

"HaHaHa... Girl, the three of you are crazy. I don't have anyone eating out of the palm of my hand. And who cares what is going on between Terrence and myself?"

"Everyone in town." The other three cousins replied in unison.

"What is going on with you and Terrence?" Ryan asked while hoping no one noticed how much makeup she was wearing. She knew Mila noticed things that were out of the ordinary quickly. Ryan was still in shock from the punch to the face she received from her boyfriend earlier today when she told him that she would be spending time with her cousins. This was the first time anything like that had happened and she would talk to him to ensure that it never happened again.

"Girl, we are just getting to know each other better and taking things one day at a time. Enjoying life and each other's company." Mila felt warm and tingly inside as she talked about Terrence. But she still couldn't help noticing the unusual amount of makeup Ryan was wearing and if she wasn't mistaken there was some slight bruising to her face. Not wanting to embarrass her cousin, Mila would talk to Ryan later in private.

"Well he would be a very nice addition to our family. Especially, since he has known all of us for many years." Desiree wanted to see her cousin happy since she knew how miserable things had been between her and Brian.

"Girl, we are not at that place yet but when we get there you all will be the first to know." Mila had a strong desire to be a wife and was hoping that this time things would work out in her relationship.

The cousins continued to eat, drink, and catch up. Their grandparents had instilled in them a strong sense of family unity and the cousins were committed to making sure their family bond was intact. They were enjoying getting to know one another as adults and friends.

"I'm so glad I had a chance to come home and catch up with all of you." Mila truly loved her family. "You all have to plan to come visit me so we can hang out with Brandon."

"Girl, you know I'm planning to come for my annual trip in November." Desiree couldn't wait to come visit in November so they could go to the outlets again. "Ryan and I will plan to come in the summer so we can visit wineries again," Renee answered for the both of them.

"Sounds like good plans to me. Please look out for my mom and granny a little more. They are getting older and you know they don't ask for help even when it is needed."

"We all decided to check on them more often and do better about going to church on Sundays," Desiree answered for the cousins.

The four paid their bill and left the restaurant to head to their respective homes. Their family bond was growing stronger each day and they would make sure the Warrington name continues to represent all that is good and respected.

# 24 WHIRLWIND

On Tuesday Mila woke to a big, home-cooked breakfast prepared by her mother. Linda served scrambled eggs, cheese grits with grilled shrimp, fried potatoes, and homemade biscuits. Mila would definitely get back on her eating plan and exercise regimen when she returned home. But for now, she was going to enjoy this succulent breakfast.

"Mom, where are you and granny headed?" Mila asked after they had finished their delicious breakfast.

"Your granny has a follow-up doctor appointment and then we are going to a special prayer service at the church."

"Okay. How has granny been feeling?"

"She seems to be doing a whole lot better. The doctor just wants to check her out from the hospital visit," Linda replied as she thought about the prayer for healing she prayed for her mother.

"Okay. Say a prayer for me at church." Mila already knew her mother prayed for her every day.

"I always do. What are you doing today?" Linda asked.

"I need to spend some time doing research for the next segment of my radio show. Later this evening I'm having dinner with Terrence."

"Honey, be careful with Terrence and don't move too fast. I don't want to see you hurt again." Linda was concerned about her daughter's happiness and was ready to see Mila married so she could have some grandbabies.

"Okay mom." Mila blew out an exasperated breath.

With her mother and grandmother gone, Mila started doing research for the next segment. Healthy self-esteem would be the focus. In her work, Mila had discovered that a lot of young girls don't feel like they have any power as females and found it difficult to name the things they liked about themselves. Mila wanted to make sure that with this segment she was able to reach at least one young lady; she hoped to help young girls see how valuable they are.

**Who Am I?**

**I am someone's daughter.**

**I am someone's sister.**

**I am someone's granddaughter.**

**I am someone's niece.**

**I am someone's cousin.**

**I am someone's friend.**

Mila would finish the poem as she would use it as a starting point to get young girls to see they are more than just the stereotypical roles portrayed in the media.

Thoughts of Terrence interrupted Mila's work. She could not wait to see him this evening and get a look at what kind of home he had. With this present visit, Mila had grown very fond of Terrence and was excited about getting to know him each day. Terrence had showered her with flowers and gifts on this visit and showed her the place she held in his life by inviting her to dinner with his colleagues and their wives. Mila felt that once Terrence moved to DC their relationship would really take off. This thought caused butterflies to flutter in Mila's stomach.

Meanwhile, Regina just received a certified letter stating that her relatives wanted her out of their family home since she has not paid them any rent. She would have to vacate the premises by May 1st.

With tears in her eyes, Regina asked, "How could I have been so stupid? If I had stayed with Terrence I wouldn't be facing eviction. I would have money and wouldn't have to worry about how I'm going to pay my bills." Regret and anger started to fill Regina causing her heart to harden even more. "How am I going to get the money? I don't have anyone to loan me the money and I don't have a job."

Regina now knew she would stop at nothing to hurt Terrence and Mila. Regina decided to put in a call to an old friend from New York she hoped would be willing to help her with this problem. She was unsure about calling Lance. Maybe he had forgiven her for the way she left. She knew that he hated Terrence, even more so now that Regina had left him and would jump at any chance to cause Terrence more embarrassment and hurt.

"Hello. I need your help ASAP! Can you meet me in my hometown to help me deal with a little matter?" Regina did not waste any time on pleasantries.

"Well... Well... Well... I've been waiting on this call for some time. You must be desperate if you're calling me. Terrence doesn't want you back does he? How soon do you need me and what is going on?" Regina's jealous ex-husband asked.

"That's not important. I need you and you're the only one I can count on. Can you be here in two weeks?"

"No, I can't. You still haven't told me what's going on."

"Terrence has started dating another woman and I want to destroy his happiness, and I want you to help me. There is also one more problem. I'm being evicted from my relatives' house and will have to move by May 1st."

"See, when you left me you thought you could just run back to Terrence. I'm sure he wants nothing to do with you. Why should I help you?"

"I know. You're right. I never should've left you. I've just never had to work and became accustomed to a certain lifestyle with Terrence so you wanting me to get a job was out of the question. So, I figured I needed to go back with the man that could give me what I wanted without my having to work for it. And you're going to help me because despite marrying me when you knew I was engaged to Terrence, as a way to get back at him for ruining your business, I know you really love me and it will definitely be worth your while." Regina was hoping that Lance would help her because she couldn't do this alone.

"HaHaHa...." Laughing, Lance replied, "I'm going to help you. But not because I love you but because I really hate Terrence and all the other pretentious people just like him that ruins people's lives with their slick business deals. I will wire you some money so that you can rent a place to live for a few months. I will not be able to come until mid-May. I'll contact you when my travel plans are set and when I get there we'll work out the details of the plan."

With that, the phone conversation ended and in Regina's mind she felt that things were finally turning in her favor.

Across town, Terrence wrapped up his business early so that he could prepare for his dinner with Mila. He had the housekeeper give the house a thorough cleaning so that everything would be perfect. Terrence filled the house with fresh flowers and strategically lit scented candles. Dinner would consist of crab cakes, a garden salad, and scalloped potatoes. For dessert, Terrence had a friend who is a chef prepare the most decadent chocolate lava cake with dulce de leche ice cream. Champagne was chilling and Terrence was geared up for a very relaxing and romantic evening with Mila.

While the food was being prepared and the champagne was chilling, Terrence decided to go upstairs and get dressed. He took a long, hot shower to get his body in a relaxed mood and so he could clear his mind. Terrence decided his gear for the evening would be khaki colored slacks with a pale pink button-down dress shirt. He couldn't wait to get this evening started with Mila.

Mila couldn't wait to see Terrence. She took extra care with her appearance this evening. She decided on a fitted, V-neck sweater dress in the most electrifying emerald green paired with high-heeled black boots. Mila went very light with her makeup and her face looked fresh and glowing. Since he had been so good to her on this visit, Mila would surprise Terrence with a striking pair of platinum cuff links. Mila grabbed her gift bag and headed to Terrence's house.

As she pulled up to the house, Mila could not believe how gorgeous Terrence's home was. The three-story colonial home featured an impressive wraparound back porch. Beautiful twinkling lights lit the way completely to the front door. Mila was not expecting this. Terrence saw Mila walking up the walkway and greeted her at the open door. "Hello beautiful."

Inside, the house was decorated in strong masculine colors of deep mahogany with blue accents. The kitchen featured granite countertops with dark cabinets. Beautiful artwork from various countries Terrence visited adorned the walls. Mila absolutely loved that the house was spotless with everything in its proper place.

"Hi Terrence. Your house is absolutely breathtaking." As she looked around, Mila admired the beautiful floral arrangements and the aroma of the vanilla scented candles.

"I'm glad you like it. Please make yourself comfortable."

While Mila was getting comfortable on the couch, Terrence poured them both glasses of champagne. Handing the glass to Mila, Terrence began a toast. "Here is to new beginnings, new love, and second chances."

"Cheers." Mila responded. "I almost forgot I have a surprise for you." Mila handed the gift bag to Terrence.

With surprise in his eyes, Terrence took the gift bag and opened the small box inside. "Mila these are nice. I needed a new pair of cuff links.

Thank you very much." Terrence grabbed Mila in a passionate embrace." I haven't received a gift from a woman that I'm dating in a very long time. Every time I wear them I will think of you."

"I'm glad you like them." Joy showed on Mila's face at the thought that Terrence was appreciative of the gift.

The couple sat down to enjoy the scrumptious meal that had been prepared for them. Mila licked her lips as the sweet, delicious chocolate from the lava cake oozed in her mouth. She was in chocolate heaven. Terrence enjoyed watching Mila as she took pleasure in devouring the magnificent dessert.

"Oh my. That was the most amazing meal." Having a mother that enjoyed cooking gave Mila a true appreciation for good food.

"I'm glad that you enjoyed it." Terrence loved a woman that wasn't afraid to eat a good meal.

"I did. Thank you for having me over. I'm having a really great time." Mila really enjoyed Terrence's company and was glad to spend time with him at his home.

"You don't have to thank me. It was my pleasure to spend time with you and wherever I have a home you are always welcome with an open invitation."

"That's good to know. And you are welcome into my home as well with an open invitation." Mila reciprocated.

Terrence grabbed Mila in a passionate, long, sensual kiss. Just as he was grabbing Mila closer, Terrence thought he saw a figure standing in the big picture window. "What the hell?" Terrence exclaimed.

"What's the matter?" Mila had a worried look on her face.

"I think someone has been watching us through the window." Terrence could have sworn it was Regina.

Terrence moved towards the window and pressed a button to turn on the light. Just as the light came on the figure, dressed in all black, dashed down the street. Terrence ran out of his front door to see if he could catch a glimpse of the figure. The figure moved quickly down the street preventing Terrence from getting a good view. But he had a firm belief that it was Regina.

## 25 IN THE EYE OF THE STORM

Time was sure flying by. It had been a month since Mila's last visit to her hometown. She and Terrence had developed an easy pattern of weekly phone conversations. Within the month Terrence would be moved to the DC area and the two could really get their relationship started. With each phone conversation, Terrence's feelings for Mila were growing stronger and more intense. On their last phone conversation, Terrence realized how much he loved Mila and this truly scared him. Terrence didn't know what to do with these feelings as he had not felt this way about a woman since his engagement and breakup with Regina.

It was now mid-April and the time had come for Terrence to move. He was excited and scared all at the same time. While Terrence loved Mila very much he wasn't sure if he was ready for a committed relationship. The pain of his broken engagement cut Terrence deeper than he realized. Unsure of what to do with his feelings for Mila, Terrence decided to focus on his move to Washington, DC instead.

The move went off without a hitch. The movers carefully packed up Terrence's home and delivered the furniture to his new penthouse apartment in the heart of downtown Washington, DC. Because of the work Terrence put into remodeling his home, the house did not have any problem being sold. The realtor in DC had been right, the penthouse was a perfect location offering a bird's eye view of the top of the Capitol Building.

Terrence couldn't wait to get settled in and start this new adventure. He would be meeting with the managers of the department he would be running to start plans of expansion and growth for their company. Terrence couldn't wait to take his department and company to the next level.

The days turned into weeks and Terrence found that he had been living in DC now for close to a month. He still had not contacted Mila and was not sure how to proceed. Mila had left several voicemail messages and sent text messages to Terrence but he couldn't bring himself to return the calls or reply to the messages. Terrence fell in love with Mila quickly and that scared him. He had also loved Regina and she had completely trampled on his heart. Terrence's pride as a man wouldn't let him be hurt by a woman like that again. But Terrence knew he had to figure something out before he lost Mila. That was not a chance he was willing to take.

"I can't believe Terrence has been in DC for over a month and he has not contacted me or returned any of my calls," Mila thought as tears pooled in her eyes. "I will not deal with this nonsense from another man. Terrence is about to find himself with me gone from his life." The walls were coming up and Mila decided she was not going to contact Terrence again.

# 26 THE BEST LAID PLANS

Back in Michigan, Regina and Lance were setting out to wreak havoc for Terrence and Mila. Lance hated Terrence. First, because of what happened in the business deal and second, because Regina went running back to Terrence when she left Lance and Lance wanted Regina all to himself. He thought once she realized that Terrence did not want her, Regina would come back to New York and be with him.

Lance was devastated when he learned that Regina had returned to the Midwest to try to win Terrence back. He was glad to receive Regina's phone call asking for his help. If all went according to his plan, Lance would have Regina all to himself, which is what he wanted.

Per Lance and Regina's plan, when Terrence and Mila came to visit for Thanksgiving, they would have a surprise ending to their trip that would leave Terrence's life in complete shambles. Regina had assured Lance that Mila and Terrence would be coming home for the Thanksgiving holiday as they both valued family and the holidays were a huge deal in both of their families. While he and Regina were planning their little surprise for Terrence and Mila, Lance was setting the stage for a plan B to ensure that Regina would be all his.

## 27 IN THE STORM

The cool spring days were starting to give way to a sunny warmth as the month of June was beginning. The change of seasons were also bringing a change in Mila's life. Terrence had now been settled in Washington, dc, for well over a month and Mila had still not heard from him. She resolved that she was not going to let this situation change her outlook on life or steal her joy from all the good things that were taking place.

Her radio show was becoming more popular with each segment and Mila was now starting to receive invitations to speak at conferences and facilitate workshops on mental health and the African-American community, especially teenage African-American females. Her grandmother's health had improved and it seemed she was given a new vitality. Mila thanked God for his blessings and favor with these two matters. Because of her faith, Mila knew more blessings were on the way. She put the issue with Terrence out of her mind and reflected on all the good things happening in her life.

One weekend while she was at the studio, Mila received an unexpected phone call. "Hello."

"Hello Mila. It's so good to hear your voice." Brian knew he should not have called Mila at the studio but he didn't know of any other way to reach her. After making all those phone calls before where Mila ended up blocking his phone number, she had also instructed all staff at the practice that no calls be put through from Brian and security knew not to let him enter the building.

"Brian, how are you?" Mila asked unsure of the reason for this call.

"Mila, I'm good. But I miss you a lot."

"Let's not get into this again. Brian, I don't have those same feelings for you anymore."

"I know. I just needed to hear your voice."

"Okay. Brian, I really am sorry that this has been difficult for you. But, you have some things that you should work through before even thinking about a relationship.

"I have started to work through them. I just thought that you could work through them with me.

"Oh Brian. With what you shared with me you need to work through those issues in therapy. Have you reached out to any of the names that I gave you?" Brian hung up without answering Mila. He did not want to go to therapy. He just wanted Mila back and everything would be okay.

"Am I being punked? Brian, won't stop calling and Terrence hasn't called." Mila just shook her head as she prepared to leave the studio for the day.

What Mila did not know was that Terrence had picked up the phone numerous times to call her but hung up before the calls went through. He had crafted dozens of text messages to send to Mila but deleted them before hitting the send button. Terrence had even thought about sending Mila hand-written letters and flowers but he just couldn't bring himself to follow through on the plans. The humiliation and devastation of the broken engagement to Regina cut Terrence deeper than he realized. Although he loved Mila and wanted to spend his life with her as her husband, Terrence felt physically ill at the thought of proposing to another woman and going through that same embarrassment. He had to figure something out soon before Mila would be gone from his life forever.

The whirlwind is starting to change direction...

# 28 THINGS EXPLAINED AND SECOND CHANCES

June turned into July and Mila still had not heard from Terrence. She had resolved that she was going to enjoy her summer, starting with this beautiful sunny day. Since they had missed the last two of their monthly outings, Mila, Karen, and Audrey decided to meet for dinner and a little girl talk. The three friends chatted about what had been going on in their lives while devouring chips and salsa as well as enchiladas and fajitas.

"Girl, I can't believe that you still have not heard from Terrence." Audrey stated with a mouth full of chips.

"I know. It just doesn't make sense. But I have cried all I'm going to cry over this nonsense." Mila did not want to ruin their great day by focusing on this issue with Terrence. "Ladies, let's toast Karen on being elected as the new president of the Northeast Region Chapter of the Association of Psychologists." The three friends shouted cheers in unison beaming with pride for their friend on such an accomplishment. As usual they had a great time fellowshipping and were out late into the evening.

As Mila was leaving the restaurant and walking to where she parked her car, Terrence was leaving a business meeting across the street from where Mila was. Mila took Terrence's breath away. He stood in a trance for a few seconds with all his love for Mila rushing back at him. Terrence called out to Mila but she kept walking as if she did not hear him.

"Oh boy. I have gone and done it now..." Terrence thought as he realized in that moment how pissed Mila was with him and how much he wanted her in his life. As Terrence was watching Mila walk away, he noticed Brian approach her. Terrence watched for a few moments to make sure that Brian did not hurt Mila and to make sure that Mila left by herself. "I'm going to do whatever it takes to get Mila back. I'm not going to lose another woman I love." Terrence vowed.

Mila saw Terrence as she was walking to her car but in her usual fashion when she is angry, she chose to ignore Terrence. Meanwhile, Brian walked up on Mila startling her out of her thinking. "Brian, what are you doing?" Mila was feeling a little shaky about Brian just popping up where she was walking.

"Mila, I'm sorry. I didn't mean to startle you. I saw you walking to your car as I was leaving the building across the street and wanted to come over and speak to you."

"It's okay. Are things good with you?"

"They are getting better. I know you are not going to believe I'm admitting this but you were right. I needed therapy like yesterday. Just know that I called a therapist referred to me by EAP at work."

"Brian, good for you. I really hope that through therapy you are able to get healthy."

"Thank you Mila. I understand what you meant when you said that I needed to work through these issues without the pressures of a committed relationship. I sincerely wish you well." Laughing, Brian added, "Don't be too hard on Terrance. I saw him yelling your name from across the street and I saw your face as I approached. I know that look. Go easy on the brother."

"Ha! Okay, Brian. I'll take that under advisement. Hey, take care of yourself and good luck with therapy." The two parted ways thankful for having known one another and grateful for the new direction their lives were taking.

Mila's thoughts turned back to Terrence. "Boy, did Terrence ever look good. His tailor-made suit fit him as it should, like it was made just for his body. Mila appreciated a man who knew how to wear a suit and Terrence knew how to wear a suit very well. But regardless of how good he looked, Mila was still very angry at Terrence, which is why she ignored him when she heard him call her name.

"Humph... I hope he doesn't think it's going to be that easy." Mila said out loud as the walls were going up. "If he ever plans to see me again, Terrence is going to have to work harder and do better than that," Mila said as she got in her car.

The next day Terrence sent the following text message to Mila:

*Mila, I've been an idiot. I'm sorry. Let's talk.*

*- Terrence*

Mila saw the text message but decided to ignore it. "He definitely better come with an explanation better than that one," Mila thought as she deleted the message.

Terrence waited two days and he still had not heard from Mila. "She must be pretty mad at me." Terrence stated to no one in particular. "Man, I don't know how I'm going to fix this one." Terrence was at a loss and had no idea how he was going to fix the mess he had made.

Although summer was the time where things generally slowed down a bit, the private practice and radio show were in full swing. At the private practice, summer was the time when groups increased as it was summer break for Mila's teenage clients. Mila's summer would also be used to do research for future segments of her radio show. Mila was so busy that she did not have time for any foolishness.

As she was leaving the radio station Saturday afternoon, Mila received another text message from Terrence. This time the message was more intense.

*Mila, my feelings for you are very strong. I got scared. I*

*don't want to lose you.*

*- With All My Love,*

*Terrence*

"Now we getting somewhere." Mila thought as she read the message. "That's much better. But Terrence still has more to do before I even consider responding to him." Once she took the emotion out of it, Mila realized that Terrence probably got scared because of his feelings and what happened the last time he loved a woman. But if their relationship was going to work, Terrence had to let go of what happened between him and Regina. Although it seemed harsh, Mila had to give Terrence some tough love so he could fully resolve his commitment issues and let go of the past. Their relationship would be the stronger for it in the long run.

This time it had been a week and Terrence still hadn't heard from Mila. "What kind of game is she playing?" Terrence shouted as he became angry at himself for the way he had treated Mila. Terrence had to pull out the big guns as Mila was not your average, ordinary woman. He had to think outside of the box on this one.

Later that week it hit Terrence. Mila loves writing in her journal and has some old school, traditional values. She is always telling people to be authentic. So, Terrence decided to be his own authentic self. He went very old school and sent Mila an old-fashioned, hand-written letter. Terrence put pen to paper and wrote Mila a letter straight from his heart. He finished the letter so that it could go out in the mail that day.

On Thursday, Mila was pleasantly surprised when she went to her mailbox and saw that she had a letter from Terrence. "Wow! I am impressed. Most people today don't recognize the value of communicating via something as personal as the hand-written letter." Mila thoroughly enjoyed receiving and sending hand-written notes. Tears pooled in Mila's eyes as she read this most beautiful letter.

> *My dearest Mila,*
>
> *I am truly sorry for the pain I have caused you. My feelings for you are so strong and I grew to be in love with you very quickly. It scared me because I know that you are the woman I want to spend my life with as my wife. The last time I thought I had found the woman that I wanted to marry, she completely ripped my heart out and trampled on it.*

As Mila read more of the letter, tears streamed down her face.

> *As a man, it is difficult to admit when you have been humiliated and your pride bruised. As a man, everything I have done since*

*that time has been to protect myself from being shamed like that again. But then you came along with your beautiful self and my heart instantly opened to you. You are not only beautiful on the outside but inside, your spirit of warmth and kindness attracts others to you and brings out the best in them. Mila, I love you very much and hope you can forgive me. I don't want to lose you. Please give me another chance.*

*- With deep and abiding love,*

*Terrence*

Mila was completely overwhelmed by Terrence's letter. No one had ever said or written anything that beautiful about her before. In that moment Mila knew she had Terrence's heart. He is the man she would spend the rest of her life with. Mila knew forgiveness was a big part of her life as a follower of Christ. In her heart, she had already forgiven Terrence. She would contact him soon so they could get started on their second chance.

Not only did Terrence send Mila the hand-written letter, but each day that week Mila received beautiful bouquets of flowers even more elaborate than the last. When she received the last bouquet, Mila sent Terrence a "thank you" note and invited him to dinner at her condo on the last Saturday in July. When Terrence received the note and invitation, he immediately called Mila to accept.

The whirlwind was now coming full circle...

The week of Mila's dinner with Terrence was here and Mila was getting nervous. She and Terrence had not spoken to or seen one another in months. Mila did not know what to expect. What she did know was that she was not ready for things to end between she and Terrence.

Mila started her preparation early in the week. She had the housekeeper come give her condo a thorough cleaning from the ceiling to the baseboards. Everything looked and smelled fresh. Mila went shopping for the groceries she would need to prepare the special dinner she had planned. For dinner Mila decided to prepare the exact same meal that she had cooked for Terrence on that first visit in February. Instead of beer for Terrence, they both would have champagne to toast this second chance.

Mid-week, Mila decided to do her favorite thing, shop. She had to find the perfect outfit. Mila decided on a little, electric blue dress with the back completely out. This was different from what she would normally wear but this was a special occasion. Her shopping trip proved to be profitable when Mila also found the perfect pair of silver stiletto sandals that complemented the dress perfectly. For jewelry, Mila decided on the diamond and platinum earrings that Terrence had given her. She wanted to keep the jewelry simple so that nothing would take away from the dress.

Friday came and went and Mila was a bundle of nerves in anticipation of this dinner with Terrence. To calm herself, Mila got a massage and settled in Friday for a relaxing evening. Just as she was about to sit down with a glass of wine her cell phone rang.

"Hey girl. You ready for your big night tomorrow?" Denise was checking up on her friend.

"Girl, I'm a bit nervous so I went and got a massage today. That seemed to calm me down. The house is immaculate, I have everything I need for the meal, and I just bought the perfect outfit. Tomorrow, I'm getting a facial and my hair done." Mila was glad Denise called her. She had a way of putting things into perspective.

"I'm confident everything will be fine tomorrow. Just keep an open mind and hear Terrence out. It took a lot of courage for him to write you that letter and open himself up like that."

"You're right. Once I took my own feelings out of it, I realized that Terrence was probably scared. I will give him the benefit of the doubt. Denise, let me call you back. Leigh is calling me."

"What's up cousin?" Mila greeted Leigh.

"Hey. I just wanted to see if you were ready for tomorrow." Leigh hoped things went well for her cousin and Terrence.

Laughing, Mila replied, "I'm ready. I have everything set for dinner and I'm most definitely going to pray before Terrence gets here so that the evening will go as God would want it to."

"Okay. Sounds like a plan. Why were you laughing?" Leigh asked her cousin.

"I was on the phone with Denise when you called in and she was asking me the same thing. I'm glad to have a caring cousin and friend."

"Girl, of course. You deserve some happiness in this relationship. Let me know how things go tomorrow."

"I will. Are things still going well with Christopher?"

"Girl, yes. We're taking it one day at a time and enjoying one another."

"Okay. That sounds good to me. I can't wait to meet him at Thanksgiving. Talk to you later." Mila stated to end the conversation.

After her two conversations, Mila decided to call it a night so that she could get enough rest for her dinner date with Terrence tomorrow night.

Meanwhile, Terrence was nervous and excited all at the same time as he was preparing for his dinner with Mila. He too went shopping and bought a new pair of tailor-made slacks and sports coat for his dinner with Mila. He would pair the charcoal grey slacks and jacket with a pale lilac shirt, remembering that purple was one of Mila's favorite colors. Terrence had also arranged for a local florist to send Mila another extravagant bouquet of flowers on Saturday just before their dinner. He also had one more surprise for Mila and could not wait to see her face.

Mila woke early Saturday morning and headed to the spa for her facial. As soon as she got up on the table, Mila could feel her body relax. The hour long facial renewed and rejuvenated Mila and gave her skin a warm glow. Tonight, Mila decided her makeup would be very light since her skin was already glowing from the facial.

After the facial, Mila headed to the salon so that her hair could get some special treatment. Her hairstylist, Paris was a true gem and took excellent care of her hair. Mila knew that when she left the salon her hair would look amazing.

"You ready for the big evening?" Paris asked after Mila came from under the dryer.

"I am. I prepped my dishes last night so when I get home all I must do is put them in the oven. My outfit is already selected and you are doing my hair."

"Sounds like you got it all under control. Please remember to enjoy the evening and don't over analyze things." Paris knew Mila could sometimes put up walls as they shared many conversations as hairstylist and client over the years and had also become good friends.

"HaHaHa... I won't. How much do I owe you for that analysis doctor?" Paris was a safe haven for Mila when she really needed to vent as the hairstylist's chair had become synonymous with the therapist's couch for Mila.

"That one is on the house. I am confident things will work out fine tonight and your hair looks gorgeous as usual."

"Girl, you did it again." Mila looked in the mirror as she admired her hair. Paris had styled Mila's cute little pixie cut in a way that perfectly shaped her face.

Mila made it home in enough time to put the dishes in the oven while she got dressed. The dress, combined with the shoes, jewelry, Mila's fresh hairstyle, and the barely there makeup; confirmed for Mila that she had made the perfect choice when she purchased this dress. Just as Mila was taking the food out of the oven, a knock sounded on the door. Mila thought it was Terrence, but was surprised when the florist was on the other side of her door with the most extravagant bouquet of flowers. It was a mixture of roses, lilies, and sunflowers. A perfect bouquet for a summer day.

Mila placed the flowers on the living room table. She decided to have a glass of wine on the balcony while she waited for Terrence. The night was beautiful. There was a slight breeze in the air that made it comfortable to be outside. The stars were twinkling and seemed to be smiling at Mila. She was in awe of God's handiwork.

Before she could get too caught up in her musings, there was another knock on the door. She was sure this was Terrence. Standing on the other side of the door was Terrence looking absolutely delectable in a charcoal grey suit that complemented his chocolate skin perfectly. And that lilac dress shirt went beautifully with that suit. Terrence too was taken by Mila's appearance. He had never seen her wear a dress like that before. The length showed off her great legs and the heels added an extra benefit making Mila's legs pop more. She looked like she didn't have on any make up and wore the diamond and platinum earrings he had given her.

"Hello Terrence." Mila finally managed to squeak out. "Come in."

"Mila, I have missed you." Terrence greeted as he caught Mila up in a warm embrace.

"I missed you too." Mila decided tonight was not a night for playing games.

"Before we go any further, Mila I want to apologize again. My actions had nothing to do with you but everything to do with my own insecurities. Our time apart gave me a lot of time to think. I also went to talk to a Christian therapist and realized that I had to learn to trust regardless of what could happen. So, God and I have been getting to know one another on a deeper level and I have been getting honest with myself about my trust in God and how I felt abandoned by him when Regina married someone else during our engagement." Terrence had to get everything out before they started their dinner. Mila, surprisingly listened patiently. As he got down on one knee with the most stunning, three-carat diamond ring in a platinum setting, Terrance said to Mila, "I love you very much. You are truly the gift that God has sent me. Would you make me proud and be my wife?"

Mila was crying as she answered with a firm, "Yes!"

Terrence grabbed Mila in a long kiss making up for all the time they missed. Dinner all but forgotten, Terrence and Mila called to share the good news with their family and friends. All the people in their lives, were so happy to hear the news and couldn't wait to celebrate with them.

The whirlwind has taken off...

# 29 THINGS TO BE THANKFUL FOR

The next month flew by for Mila and Terrence as they started planning for their upcoming wedding. They were planning for a Spring wedding and both of their parents couldn't be more happy and excited for their children. This would be the celebration and wedding of the century.

When Regina heard of Terrence and Mila's engagement, she was fuming and realized that her plan had to be set in motion quickly. Regina became undone when she read the announcement in the paper detailing Terrence and Mila's courtship and engagement. "I can't lose Terrence this way!" Regina exclaimed while sobbing. "I never should've let him go in the first place. But I'm going to do everything in my power to get him back." With that Regina vowed to stop at nothing to destroy the future Terrence and Mila were planning.

Meanwhile, the months were flying by. Terrence and Mila decided that it would be best for Mila to move into Terrence's penthouse and they would rent out her condo. The month of September was a flurry of activity with Mila packing up her home and moving into the penthouse with Terrence. Mila donated a large portion of her furniture and kitchen items to charity but made sure that all her crystal, paintings, and sorority items came with her to her new home. Terrence had a new closet installed for all of Mila's clothes, shoes, and jewelry. As her items were being unpacked Mila was starting to feel like this was her new home.

The two settled into an easy pattern of domestic life over the next month and adjusted to sharing a home with one another. Terrence was looking forward to sharing his life with Mila and she was looking forward to being his wife. The couple decided that they would enter premarital counseling to ensure that their marriage would start off on a solid foundation.

October turned into November and the start of Mila's favorite time of the year with the upcoming holiday season. Mila felt like there was a magic energy in the air at this time of year and could not wait to celebrate the holiday with Terrence and their families. This November Terrence and Mila's families had planned an engagement party for them on their visit for Thanksgiving.

Terrence and Mila had decided to leave the Tuesday before Thanksgiving to head to their hometown for the holiday. Leaving on Tuesday would ensure that they beat the holiday travel crowd and give them extra time to check out venues for their wedding. "Honey, I'm so excited for this Thanksgiving holiday and look forward to sharing many holidays with you," Mila stated as she gazed at Terrence with eyes full of love.

"I can't wait either. I'm going to leave all the planning to you. Just tell me who to make the checks out to," Terrence said with a chuckle in his voice.

"I don't have a problem with that. But it's not just my wedding and I want your input with the planning." Mila wanted to ensure that Terrence was included in the planning of their wedding and felt like he had a say in the decisions surrounding their special day.

"Okay. I will make sure to give you my opinion but let's finish packing. The car will be here soon to take us to the airport."

With that the couple finished their packing and headed to the airport to board their plane. Once they made it to their hometown, the two did not have time to breathe as they ran from venue to venue with both of their mothers in hopes of finding the right location for their wedding. The whole day, both Terrence and Mila had the sense that someone was following them, and it wasn't Regina.

Regina and Lance went over their plan again. They would wait for an opportunity when Terrence and Mila were apart and Lance would grab Mila giving her a lethal dosage of chloroform and stage her body like it was a random robbery and assault. They had decided to leave her body at Lake Michigan since that was an area most people knew that

Mila often went.

Since their hometown was small, it was not hard for Regina to find out where Terrence and Mila's engagement party would be held. The miserable couple would hide out in an area of the venue where no one could see them and wait for the perfect opportunity to strike and snatch Mila. If things went per their plan, it would be the end of Mila's life and Terrence would be left devastated. What Regina, did not tell Lance was that this would also leave her to console the grieving Terrence. In her twisted mind, Regina thought this would guarantee that she would get her fiancé back.

Thanksgiving Day had arrived and Regina had not seen Lance all day. She was starting to get nervous as his behavior had been very erratic since Terrence and Mila arrived in town. Terrence and Mila had decided to spend the holiday with both of their families at the Warrington home. This day would be spent being grateful for all their blessings to include their upcoming wedding and love's promise of a beautiful life together.

Before they went to dinner with their families, Terrence and Mila decided to serve food at the local homeless shelter to give to those less fortunate and show their gratitude for their blessings. On their way to the shelter, Terrence and Mila noticed that the same car had been following them for a few miles on this stretch of road leading to the shelter. As they were approaching a very dangerous curve on the road, the car sped up coming within inches of running Terrence and Mila off the road. Terrence managed to safely maneuver the car, barely missing a collision with the other car.

"Terrence what is happening?" Mila shouted as fear gripped her.

"Babe, stay calm. I think someone is trying to run us off the road." Just as he said this, the other car, driven by Lance, came at the car Terrence and Mila were riding in at 90 miles per hour even though the speed limit was only 25 miles per hour for safety. Terrence said a prayer to God asking him to keep him and Mila safe and protected from the harm that was facing them. Just as he said the prayer, Terrence was able to narrowly escape impact with the other car by swerving an inch to the left. Lance's car swerved at the high speed and began to roll. The car then hit the embankment and rolled down into the ditch.

As they thanked God for keeping them safe, Terrence and Mila got out of their car to check on the driver in the other car. Within that moment, they heard a loud boom and saw the car going up in flames. Terrence called the police and Mila called their families to tell them what happened.

The police and their families showed up at the same time. Both mothers' eyes were filled with tears as they were grateful that neither of their children had been hurt. Terrence and Mila gave their statements to the police. Because the car and driver had been burned badly in the crash it would take some time before the police knew who had tried to run them off the road. Out of the corner of his eye, Terrence could see Regina off in the distance and knew in that instant that she had something to do with them being run off the road.

"What is wrong with that fool Lance? That was not the plan. He was only supposed to kidnap Mila and leave her for dead at Lake Michigan." Regina was starting to panic. She realized that once his identity was confirmed, she would be linked back to Lance and this accident. She hightailed it back to the house she was sharing with Lance, grabbed the cash that he had stashed in the house, and left town without a word to anyone.

That Thanksgiving holiday Terrence, Mila, and their families had a lot to be thankful for and were reminded life can be caught up in a whirlwind of love that will eventually lead to love's promise.

# ABOUT THE AUTHOR

Dr. Daphne L. King is the creator behind Writings by Daphne, the platform she uses for writing/publishing, life coaching, and speaking engagements. She is also the Director of Program Operations for Transition Solutions Enterprises, Inc. and completed a doctorate in Education in Counseling Psychology from Argosy University in Washington, DC. Dr. King was born and raised in Muskegon Heights, MI where she received her foundation to live life at its fullest by a very supportive and loving family.

Daphne's first book, a book of poetry, "Love Heals All Wounds" was the culmination of years of writing and putting feelings on paper. Daphne's writing is a gift that she has been blessed with by God and is one that she has begun to fully nurture.

Writing or journaling has always been a way for Daphne to express her feelings and communicate the stage she is in at certain points of time in her life. Dr. King currently lives in Fairfax County, Virginia right outside of Washington, DC. She is actively involved in the ministry of Marlboro Meadows Baptist Church, as well as Alpha Kappa Alpha Sorority, Inc., Xi Omega Chapter. In her spare time, Daphne enjoys reading, shopping, traveling, and spending time with friends and family.

In this book, Regina suffered from untreated mental illness that impacted her outlook on life and the decisions she made. We also saw that Brian needed to seek out therapy to help him deal with a troubled childhood that was plagued by his mother's mental health issues and abuse. Additionally, Tim Warrington has some demons that he is dealing with from being in combat that led him to have periods where he didn't have any contact with his family.

Good mental health is just as important as good physical health. So many times, we ignore our mental health and don't seek proper help when we are dealing with difficult times. Often, our veterans do not receive proper mental health treatment when they come back from war leading to various kinds of problems adjusting to civilian life.

Some indications that you or someone you know may need to seek out a professional mental health counselor is if you are experiencing debilitating sadness that has occurred over a significant period of time, you are withdrawing from family and friends, your sleep pattern has significantly changed, your appetite has significantly changed, or you have an increase in substance use. There is no shame in seeking out help from a mental health professional. You can seek help from your local mental health agency, the National Alliance on Mental Illness (NAMI) www. nami.org 800-950-NAMI, Suicide Prevention Lifeline 800-273-8255, or www.depression.org.